THE CLUE IN THE DIARY

NANCY and her friends, George and Bess, are returning from a country carnival when they witness the explosion and burning of a beautiful country mansion. Fearing its occupants may be trapped in the blazing building, they rush to the rescue—and unexpectedly find themselves confronted with a mystery that seems to be insoluble.

The first clue is an anonymous diary, its entries in a handwriting difficult to decipher. Even more puzzling are the technical drawings and chemical formulas contained in its pages.

Who dropped the diary near the burning house? Was it the gaunt stranger Nancy glimpsed running away from the flaming structure? What was he doing there? And does he know the whereabouts of Felix Raybolt, an unscrupulous dealer in patents, who has not been seen since his home burned? Or did Raybolt die in the fire?

Fire investigators believe that the destructive explosion and fire may not have been an accident—but an act of revenge. Evidence mounts against Joe Swenson, an inventor who was swindled by "Foxy Felix." Prompted by her affection for Mr. Swenson's five-year-old daughter Honey, the young detective makes a desperate effort to exonerate the inventor of the suspicion of arson. How she accomplishes this makes another exciting Nancy Drew mystery.

"It's evidence against him!" Nancy said
to herself. "He can't destroy it!"

NANCY DREW MYSTERY STORIES

The Clue in the Diary

BY CAROLYN KEENE

NEW YORK

Grosset & Dunlap

PUBLISHERS

PRINTED IN THE UNITED STATES OF AMERICA

Contents

The Clue in the Diary

CHAPTER I

A Suspicious Stranger

"A PENNY for your thoughts, Nancy Drew," said George Fayne. "You've been staring into space for nearly two minutes!"

"And missing all this good food!" added blond Bess Marvin. The slightly plump, pretty girl reached for a third sandwich.

"George," said Nancy to Bess's slim, short-haired cousin, who enjoyed her boy's name, "I'm worried about that darling Swenson child and her mother. I wish we could do something to help them."

"You mean," said Bess, "find Mr. Swenson, or the money his wife told us he had promised to send?"

"Yes," Nancy answered. "It's very mysterious, since apparently he has been away for some time. I wonder if his letters—containing money orders —were stolen."

1

"That's a federal offense," George said grimly.

The three girls, seated beneath a spreading roadside maple tree, were enjoying a picnic supper. The peaceful spot was halfway between their home town of River Heights and Sandy Creek, where they had attended a popular annual carnival.

Bess chuckled. "If there's a thief around, Nancy will capture him!" She reached for a deviled egg. "Count me in to help with the sleuthing—if it's not too dangerous."

"I wouldn't count on its *not* being dangerous," said George. "You know Nancy."

The young sleuth smiled at this remark, but in a moment became serious again. All of Nancy's friends agreed that she possessed an intangible appealing quality which people never forgot.

Nancy was pretty in a distinctive way. Her eyes were blue, her hair titian blond. She expressed her opinions firmly, but did not force them on others. Nancy's abilities of leadership were welcome and depended upon in any group.

With Bess and George, Nancy had made the drive to Sandy Creek in her convertible. From the breath-taking "Whip" to the airplane swings, they had left nothing untried, and true to her reputation, Nancy had unearthed an adventure.

Her attention had been drawn to a little girl and her mother among the carnival crowd. They had been looking on wistfully, but had taken no part in the fun. Nancy and her friends had sensed that the mother could not afford admission tickets. On impulse, the girls had invited them to go along on several rides.

The three had fallen in love with five-year-old Honey. She was a bright and appealing child in spite of the fact that she looked undernourished. Her dress, though neat, was faded.

"Honey was so adorable," Nancy remarked, half to herself.

"Yes, she certainly was," Bess agreed.

"We must see the Swensons again," Nancy said thoughtfully. "I can't bear to think of that little girl's going without the things she needs. We'll visit the Joe Swenson family someday soon at their home. You wrote down the address, didn't you, Bess?"

"Yes."

"It won't be easy to do things for Mrs. Swenson," George predicted. "That woman is proud. You can see that."

"I know," Nancy admitted. "She didn't like our paying for everything at the carnival, but for Honey's sake she allowed it."

Bess, gazing toward the west, observed that the sun was sinking below the horizon. "We'd better be on our way," she declared.

The girls arose and put the food wrappings into the car. They had pulled into a side road. Now Nancy carefully steered the convertible over the rough road to the main highway, then headed for River Heights.

After the first few miles, Bess slumped down and wearily leaned her head back against the seat, while gazing out the window. "Nice homes along this road," she observed presently.

"Mostly country estates," George added.

"Look at that large white house on the hill." Nancy pointed toward one with spacious grounds and a woods behind it. "Isn't it a dream? The lawns are so well kept. Just my idea of a country place."

"Wonder who owns it?" George asked.

Nancy had no chance to reply. Suddenly there was a tremendous explosion, and in an instant the lovely white house on the hillside burst into flames! Tongues of fire leaped from the windows and doors.

"There may be people trapped inside!" Nancy cried out. "We must help them!"

She drove frantically toward the burning house, pressing the automobile horn incessantly, hoping to attract the attention of neighboring residents. As the girls passed other vehicles, Bess and George shouted and pointed toward the house on the hill.

"We'll need all the help we can get," Nancy said grimly, "if anyone is to be rescued."

The convertible swung into the driveway and headed up the hill toward the burning building.

"There may be people trapped inside!"
Nancy cried out

At a glance it was apparent to the girls that the house could not be saved. Nancy stopped the car and the three jumped out.

"If there are people trapped inside," George exclaimed as they dashed toward the house, "how can we ever save them?"

The girls scanned the windows anxiously but could see no one. Already the smoke was thick and the heat warned them that they could not enter—at least, not from the front.

"I'll try the back," Nancy told the cousins. "The smoke may not be so dense there. You'd better take the car to the nearest house and phone the fire department."

As Bess and George hurried off, Nancy quickly rounded the house, only to be met by a heavy cloud of smoke being carried by the wind. It made her cough and choke, and for a moment her eyes burned so that she could barely see.

Nancy started forward again, then halted abruptly as she caught sight of a man about to crawl through the back hedge. He seemed to be running away from the burning building. Did this mean he might have set the house on fire?

"Stop!" Nancy cried.

The man turned his head and in the glare of the fire she caught a momentary but clear glimpse of his face. He was very blond, ruddy complexioned, and square jawed. Instantly he whirled, crawled through the thick hedge, and vanished.

"His actions were those of a guilty person," Nancy thought. Who was he? she wondered. Nancy saw him again when he stood up behind the hedge. The man was tall and gaunt, and poorly dressed.

"He doesn't look like a criminal," she thought. "But his identification might prove vitally important to the authorities."

Nancy had an instinctive talent for detective work. She was the only child of Carson Drew, a widely known lawyer. Mrs. Drew had passed away when Nancy was a very young child, and daughter and father had become close companions. They often helped each other on cases.

The first mystery Nancy had solved was *The Secret of the Old Clock,* involving her in a dangerous search for a missing will. Since then, she had successfully tackled other unusual cases. Nancy's most recent adventure, centering around a strange white-robed clan, cleared up *The Mystery at Red Gate Farm.*

As Nancy stood staring after the stranger who had disappeared into the woods, she heard fire engines clang up to the house. She dashed to the front and met George and Bess, breathless from running. Neighbors were arriving from all directions, some on foot, others in automobiles. The sight of the burning building had attracted passing motorists, and the driveway was quickly jammed with cars.

The firemen realized at once that nothing could be saved. By playing heavy streams of water on the house, the firemen barely succeeded in keeping the blaze from spreading to the outbuildings.

"What a shame such a beautiful home had to burn!" Bess remarked as the girls watched the firemen work. "I—I hope the owners aren't in there."

A woman who was standing nearby turned to answer. "The Raybolts' house has been closed all summer, so I guess no one is inside."

"I hope not," Nancy murmured.

"So Mr. Raybolt doesn't know of his loss," Bess commented. "What a blow it will be!"

"Oh, I guess *Mrs.* Raybolt can stand it," the woman returned indifferently. "Her husband has plenty of money."

"You know them then?" Nancy questioned.

The woman shook her head. "Only by reputation. I live near here, but the Raybolts were never neighborly."

"Have they a large family?" Nancy asked.

"No, there are only the two of them, and they're a pair! Mrs. Raybolt thinks she's a bit too good for anyone around here." Nancy and her friends gathered that the owners of the ruined house were far from well liked.

In spite of the desperate efforts of the firemen, it was impossible to keep the blaze under control. Nancy noted with alarm that the wind was steadily rising and veering to the north. At any moment the outbuildings might ignite.

"Oh!" Bess cried. "Look! The roof of the house is falling in!"

A wave of heat drove the girls back a few steps and unexpectedly a thick cloud of smoke blew toward them. Nancy choked and gasped. When the smoke did not clear away she ran to escape it.

Bess and George had scattered in opposite directions, and when Nancy looked about for them, they were not in sight. Before she could call their names, the wind brought another cloud of dense smoke swirling down upon her.

Blindly Nancy stumbled toward the driveway where it curved around the rear of the house. She ran straight into a small wooden structure, and the impact nearly knocked her over. As the smoke drifted away, she could not help laughing. "Only a doghouse!" she thought. "Lucky there was no mean dog in it to attack me!"

As Nancy started back to the driveway she caught sight of a small leather-covered book lying a few feet from the doghouse. Eagerly Nancy snatched it up.

She decided that the book must have been dropped that day. Otherwise, the cover would have been ruined by a heavy rain the previous night. Nancy was struck with a sudden idea. When running across the back lawn of the burning house, the mysterious tall stranger must have passed this very spot. Could he have dropped the book?

"Perhaps I've stumbled on a clue!" Nancy thought excitedly.

CHAPTER II

An Excitable Driver

NANCY thrust the little book into the pocket of her sports dress. She resisted the temptation to examine it on the spot, for wind-whipped sparks from the fire were flying in every direction.

She glanced about quickly but could not locate her friends. Bess and George were lost in the crowd.

A flying ember narrowly missed Nancy. "I'd better be on the move!" she warned herself, observing that the wind had shifted, and was blowing toward the driveway.

Nancy saw with alarm that a patch of dry grass had flared up very close to the parked automobiles. Several men leaped forward, and began stamping on the flames, but the burning embers were dropping everywhere.

Nancy hurried toward her convertible. "I'd better move it!" she thought.

Suddenly Nancy stopped and stared in astonishment. A strange young man was climbing into her car. The next instant he started the motor!

"Bess and George must have left the key in the ignition lock!" Nancy said to herself, rushing forward, "Is he trying to steal my car?"

Nancy reached the convertible just as the self-appointed driver started to back it down the driveway, skillfully avoiding the other vehicles which were parked at various angles nearby.

"Your car?" he inquired with a disarming smile as Nancy ran alongside the convertible. "I thought I'd move it out of the danger zone."

"Thank you," Nancy murmured a trifle uncertainly. "I think it will be safe right here unless the wind changes again."

The young man pulled as close to the edge of the drive as possible. He was about nineteen, Nancy decided, surveying him critically. His hair was dark and slightly curly, his eyes whimsical and friendly. He wore a college fraternity pin.

Nancy was still wary, nevertheless. The stranger must have read her thoughts, for he slid from behind the wheel and with a cheerful nod of farewell disappeared into the crowd.

"I don't know what to make of him," Nancy thought in bewilderment. "He looks like a nice person—and yet, appearances can be deceiving. Oh, dear, where *are* Bess and George?"

At that very moment she caught sight of the cousins hurrying toward her. "We thought we'd lost you for good," George declared as the girls climbed into the car. "Look at my dress, will you! I stumbled over a stone and landed flat!"

"And I'm nearly suffocated from smoke!" Bess said weakly.

"I think it's time we start for home," Nancy declared. "If this wind keeps up, the fire will last for hours. We've done all we can to help."

Bess and George readily agreed to leave, and it seemed that dozens of other spectators felt the same way. The wind had increased in velocity, posing a fresh threat to all the cars in the vicinity of the burning house. Many vehicles crowded into the narrow driveway leading to the main road, and soon a traffic jam resulted.

Horns blasted noisily. Fenders scraped and angry words were hurled back and forth.

"Why *don't* they stop honking?" George exclaimed impatiently. "It doesn't help a bit. We'll be here all night!"

Inch by inch Nancy's car progressed toward the main road, with the congested traffic beginning to unsnarl itself. Then suddenly a new shower of sparks descended upon the automobiles nearest the house. The drivers of these cars, anxious to get away from the flying embers, tried to force their way into the line of traffic ahead by crowding in out of turn.

"Look out!" George cried suddenly. "That man is going to hit us!"

Nancy was trapped. The driver apparently had lost control of his sedan. *Crash!* It plowed into the rear of Nancy's convertible with an impact that gave the three girls a severe jolt.

They sat stunned for a moment, but fortunately none of them was injured. Nancy leaped out, and saw at a glance that her car had been badly damaged. One fender was crumpled, the rear lights were smashed, and the bumper dragged on the ground.

Her first inclination was to tell the driver what she thought of the incompetent way he had handled his car. But the man was instantly apologetic, and obviously so shaken that Nancy relented. She wrote down his name, address, and license number.

"I'd also like the name of your insurance company, Mr. Weston," Nancy told him.

The thin, wiry man became more flustered than ever. "I—I'm terribly sorry. I'm in such a state of confusion, I can't even remember the name. And I don't have the company's card with me."

It was finally decided that he would notify his agent about the accident, and Nancy would contact Mr. Weston after she had learned the total cost of repairs.

"The bill will be taken care of, believe me," the man assured Nancy. "I'll collect my wits, once I'm home. No more driving for me in dangerous spots. Doctor says I shouldn't drive, anyway. Too nervous."

With a final apology, the excitable Mr. Weston retreated to his sedan, and after much difficulty, maneuvered his way past Nancy's disabled car.

"He sure *shouldn't* drive!" George exclaimed. "That man's a menace!"

Bess looked at Nancy. "You don't think he was putting on an act about the insurance, do you?" she said. "You'll have a huge repair bill!"

"I know," Nancy returned. "Don't worry. You may be sure Mr. Weston will pay it—one way or another. Right now, we must get out of this mess!"

"How'll we get home with the bumper dragging?" George questioned.

"We'll have to find a garage," Nancy said as the girls seated themselves once more in the convertible.

Nancy started again and slowly moved forward. George groaned. "The rear of this car sounds as if it were about to fall out!"

Just then Nancy was forced to a halt by the bumper-to-bumper traffic. The girls might have been held up indefinitely on the hillside, but fortunately a young man stepped in to act as a traffic policeman. In a few minutes he had the line of cars moving steadily. By the time the girls reached the exit of the Raybolt grounds, the tangle was fairly well straightened out.

To Nancy's surprise, she saw that the young man was the same one who had moved her convertible a short time before.

"I did misjudge him," she chided herself. "He *was* only trying to help and didn't have the slightest intention of stealing my car. How silly of me!"

On the main road at last, Nancy pulled off to the side to learn the full extent of the damage to her car. While she was surveying the rear axle doubtfully, the young man came over and offered his services.

"I'm Ned Nickerson," he declared with a warm smile. "Anything I can do?"

"Yes," Nancy said. "Please tell us how far it is to the nearest service garage. Another car banged into mine—as you can see."

"There's a garage at Mapleton—about two miles away."

"I wonder if my car will hold together even that short distance."

"It should, if your axle isn't badly damaged."

"But with the bumper dragging—"

"I'll fix that. I might as well pull it off entirely."

With a strong, deft twist, Ned Nickerson tore the bumper loose and placed it in the trunk compartment.

"Look here!" he proposed suddenly. "I'm going to Mapleton—my home's there. I'll keep close behind your car and push it if necessary."

"Thanks a lot," Nancy said gratefully, "but I don't like to trouble you."

"No trouble at all. Glad to do it."

She smiled and introduced herself and the other girls.

When the four reached the Mapleton garage, a mechanic inspected the convertible and said, "I'm afraid I can't have this car ready for at least an hour, miss. Even at that I can't touch the fender or taillights. You'll have to leave the car until tomorrow or else get the work done at your home garage. The best I can do now is fix you up so you can make it home."

"An hour, you say?" Nancy asked. "I suppose we'll have to wait, but we're in a hurry to get to River Heights."

"How about my treating to ice-cream sodas while we wait," Ned suggested. "There's a drug store across the street."

The girls accepted and phoned their homes about the delay. The hour passed quickly. After a gay get-acquainted session, Ned accompanied Nancy, Bess, and George back to the garage.

"I'll have the car ready in ten minutes," the mechanic promised.

The young people went outside and chatted about the recent events. But soon their attention was attracted by a group of men standing under a nearby street lamp discussing the Raybolt fire.

" 'Pears mighty strange to me that a fire would

start when the place ain't been occupied all summer," one elderly man commented.

"Old Raybolt deserved to be burnt out," another added. "The skinflint! He'd steal a crust of bread from a starvin' child!"

"Wouldn't surprise me if he burned the place down himself—to get the insurance," a third voice chimed in. "I wouldn't put it past Foxy Felix!"

Nancy and her friends heard no more, for at that moment the mechanic announced that her car was ready. "It's the best I could do on such short notice," he told her. "Better have your garage man give it a general overhauling when you get home."

While Ned backed the convertible out of the shop, Nancy paid the mechanic and asked him for a receipted bill. She explained that she wished to collect from the motorist who had crashed into her.

"I take it Mr. Raybolt isn't very well liked around here," Nancy remarked to Ned as she relieved him at the wheel.

"No, he isn't," Ned declared emphatically. "He's about as popular as a tiger who's escaped from a circus!"

"Apparently they call him Foxy Felix."

"Yes, and from all one hears about him the name is deserved." An odd expression flashed across Ned's face and he looked intently through the window at Nancy. "I also wonder what could have started that fire! You know, I have a sneaking suspicion it didn't start by accident."

"So have I," Nancy returned with a meaningful grin.

Before Ned could question her, she quickly but graciously thanked him for his help, then drove away.

"You girls haven't seen the last of me," the young man called gaily after them. "I know the road to River Heights. Don't be surprised if I follow it one of these days!"

CHAPTER III

The Diary

"DID you hear what Ned Nickerson said?" Bess Marvin teasingly asked Nancy, who pretended to be intent upon her driving. "You've made a hit, all right!"

"Hit!" Nancy retorted. "The only thing that was hit is the back of my car. Won't Dad be shocked when he sees the wreck I'm bringing home!"

"She's trying to change the subject!" George chortled. "Look at her blush. You can tell she likes him."

"Why shouldn't I?" Nancy defended herself stanchly. "Ned Nickerson certainly helped us out of a tight spot."

"He's handsome, too." Bess giggled. "And what a soulful expression in those big blue eyes of his when he looks at our Nancy!"

"Were they blue? I thought they were—"

Nancy broke off as she realized that Bess had deliberately trapped her. "All right, you win!" She laughed. "But just to get even I've half a mind not to tell you what I discovered while we were at the fire."

"Oh, come on!" George pleaded.

"All right. I'll forgive you this time."

Nancy was eager to relate what she had observed at the Raybolt grounds, for she wondered if her chums would interpret the incident the same way. She told them of the suspicious, gaunt-looking stranger who had run away from the burning house.

"That man must have set it on fire!" Bess declared. "Otherwise, why would he be afraid to answer when you called?"

"He might have been a tramp who went into the house for shelter," George suggested thoughtfully, "and started the fire accidentally—perhaps from a lighted cigarette."

"I thought of that," Nancy admitted, "but it seems to me if the fire had begun that way it would have burned more slowly. Remember the sound of an explosion and how the house appeared to blaze up all at once?"

"That's true," George said, then added, "Guess we'll have to wait for the investigators' reports."

There was not much traffic that evening, and the girls reached River Heights in good time.

"There's Mother out on the porch!" Bess

cried as they drew up before the Marvin residence. "She's been watching for us."

Next, Nancy dropped George at her home and then drove to the Drew house. As she pulled into the driveway, her father and Hannah Gruen, the housekeeper, came rushing out. Mr. Drew was tall and distinguished looking. The housekeeper, pleasantly plump, had a motherly expression.

"Are you all right?" they asked Nancy in unison.

"Yes, indeed, but I'm afraid my car will never look the same again."

"I don't care about the car," Mr. Drew said to his daughter, "as long as you're not hurt." Then he relaxed and asked, "The question now is how big a lawsuit will I have on my hands?"

"Suit? Oh, I see. You think I backed into another car. Don't worry. Another car ran into *mine*. I have the driver's name and license number. I'm to get in touch with him and let him know my repair cost."

As they entered the house, Mrs. Gruen went to the kitchen, while Nancy and her father turned into the living room.

"Tell me more about the fire," Mr. Drew urged. "Whose house is it?"

"The owner is Felix Raybolt."

"Felix Raybolt! Foxy Felix!" Mr. Drew exclaimed.

"Do you know him?" Nancy asked, surprised.

"Only by reputation—which isn't enviable. As a matter of fact, just today I accepted a case for a client, Arnold Simpson, who wants to sue Mr. Raybolt. He tells me there are many other people who would like to do so."

"What is Mr. Raybolt like, Dad?"

"Very shrewd, and very unfriendly. I understand he's wealthy."

"How did he make his money?"

"He deals in patents, and I've heard he made fortunes on some of them."

"You mean, Mr. Raybolt invents things?" Nancy questioned.

"No, he buys patents from inventors and cashes in on their ideas."

"Is that legitimate?"

"Yes, he has a right to buy a patent and make a profit from it. The unfair part is that Raybolt takes advantage of the inventor by verbally promising to pay him a royalty after he has marketed the device.

"In fact, that is the complaint of my client. He told me that Raybolt purchased a patent from him covering a certain part for an automatic elevator at a ridiculously low figure, then sold the patent to a manufacturing concern for a much higher sum. When Mr. Simpson reminded Raybolt of his promise, Foxy Felix turned him down —practically laughed in his face."

"No wonder people dislike Mr. Raybolt,"

Nancy remarked. "I suppose there are certain persons who might have set fire to his house out of pure revenge."

"Undoubtedly."

After a late, light supper, Nancy admitted being tired. She said good night to her father and Hannah and went upstairs.

As she slipped off her dress, the red leather booklet which she had found on the Raybolt estate dropped to the floor. Nancy snatched it up with an exclamation of eagerness.

"This may furnish the clue I need!" she thought. "At any rate, I have an idea it will prove interesting. I'll read it this very night!"

Nancy forgot that she was tired and sleepy. Undressing hastily, she adjusted the reading lamp and took the book to bed with her.

"This is a diary," she decided, noting that each entry was preceded by a date. "Perhaps it contains the owner's name and address."

Settling herself comfortably against the pillow, Nancy opened the loose-leaf booklet. She stared in surprise at the first entry. The page was filled with baffling words, written in a foreign language.

She studied the text. Finally two familiar words struck her eye. "*Adjö*—good-by. And *god vän*—good friend. Swedish!" Nancy murmured, recalling that a schoolmate of hers, a girl from Sweden, had often spoken these words in her native tongue.

"Oh, dear, I can't read the rest of it!" The young detective groaned.

She rapidly leafed through the pages. All the entries were in Swedish except the last few, which were written in cramped English.

Nancy held the diary closer to the reading lamp and tried to make out the words. But it was a discouraging task, since the letters had been run together in an indistinguishable fashion. She did manage to decipher a few scattered phrases, but try as she would, Nancy could not figure out a single entire sentence.

"How exasperating!" she thought impatiently. "This diary may contain a valuable clue, but I can't read it!"

The notations in Swedish were in larger handwriting than those in English. Nancy felt sure the diary belonged to a man, for though the writing was small and cramped, the characters were bold. She reflected, too, that if the little journal *had* been dropped by the stranger whom she had seen running away from the fire, it was all the more important for her to learn his name and what he had written in the diary.

"I'll have to find someone who can read Swedish," she said to herself. "If only Karen were here!" But Nancy's former schoolmate had returned to her native country with her family.

With that thought Nancy lowered her pillow, put out the light, and the next instant was asleep.

It seemed only minutes later when she was awakened by the ringing of the telephone in the hall. The sun was shining through the windows and from the angle of the rays Nancy guessed that it must be after nine o'clock. Hannah, knowing that she was exhausted, had let her oversleep.

With a guilty start, Nancy jumped out of bed. Before she could open the door, Mrs. Gruen came in. "Good morning, Nancy. A young man wishes to speak to you on the phone."

"I'll be there in a jiffy. Don't let him escape!"

Thrusting her feet into dainty black-and-gold slippers and snatching up her dressing robe, Nancy hurried to the hall telephone.

"Hope I didn't get you out of bed," a low, pleasant voice came over the wire. "This is Ned —Ned Nickerson."

"Oh!" Nancy stammered, taken completely by surprise.

"You probably think I'm rushing things a bit," Ned went on, "but I picked up a ring at the Raybolts' this morning, and thought it might be yours."

"I didn't wear one yesterday," Nancy returned, finding her voice at last. "George or Bess might have lost one, though."

"The ring couldn't be theirs. It has a 'D' on it."

"Did you find the ring in the ashes?" Nancy questioned with rising interest.

"No. The firemen and police won't let anyone

go near the ruins. I found the signet ring near the hedge back of the house."

There was a brief moment of silence as Nancy mulled this over. Then she asked quickly, "Does that ring bear a Swedish inscription? If it does, I may have a clue to the owner."

She was thinking of the stranger she suspected of being the owner of the mysterious diary— the man who had vanished behind the Raybolt hedge.

"There is an inscription in a foreign language, but I can't read it," Ned told her. "Say! Would you like to see the ring?"

"Love to," Nancy confessed. "It may furnish a clue. But shouldn't the ring be turned over to the police?"

Ned did not agree. "I believe, at least for the time being, it's a case of 'Finders Keepers.' The ring was a good distance away from the fire area."

"All right, then. I *am* eager to see it."

"If you'll let me, I'll drop around tonight at eight and bring the ring along," Ned offered.

"Good."

After Ned had hung up, Nancy fairly danced back into the bedroom. She sent one slipper flying toward the bed, and the other into the far corner of the room. The young sleuth attempted to convince herself that her jubilant spirits were the result of Ned's discovery. The ring might be a clue to the identity of the person who had set the

Raybolt house on fire. Bess and George, she knew, would have interpreted her reaction very differently!

As soon as she had dressed, Nancy picked up the diary and placed it in her top bureau drawer for safekeeping.

"I wish I had time to go somewhere and have it translated right now," she thought regretfully, "but it's late and I must take my car to the garage."

Nancy hurried downstairs to the kitchen. Mr. Drew had already eaten breakfast and left for his office. Hannah Gruen uncovered a hot plate on the stove.

"Mm, blueberry muffins," Nancy said. After biting into one, she added, "Oh, this is extra delicious." As she ate, Nancy told the housekeeper about wanting the diary translated.

"But kept confidential, I suppose," Mrs. Gruen remarked. "It's not often that I can help you on a mystery, Nancy, but this time I believe I can."

CHAPTER IV

The Initialed Ring

"OH, HANNAH, that's wonderful!" Nancy exclaimed. "But don't tell me *you* can read Swedish."

"I wish I could. The person to translate the diary is our old Swedish bakery friend, Mr. Peterson. He has moved his shop to the other side of town."

"Oh, I remember Mr. Peterson," said Nancy with a chuckle. "When I was a little girl, and you and I went there, I used to wheedle tarts and cookies from him."

"And always get them," Mrs. Gruen replied, a twinkle in her eye. "You were his favorite customer. I'm sure that he'll be glad to translate the diary for you."

Nancy was delighted at the prospect of seeing kindly Oscar Peterson again.

"Hannah, that's a wonderful idea! I'll go to the bakery first chance I have. Right now, I must have my car fixed."

Nancy took the convertible to a garage downtown. The mechanic promised to have it ready sometime the following afternoon. Then Nancy walked slowly homeward. Suddenly Nancy heard her name called. Turning, she saw Bess and George hurrying to meet her.

"You must be daydreaming about Ned!" cried George as the cousins swung into step beside her. "We shouted three times."

"Sorry." Nancy laughed.

" 'Fess up, now. Weren't you thinking about him?" Bess prodded.

An animated expression came over Nancy's face. Her eyes danced mischievously as she told her bit of news.

"Ned phoned this morning before I was up."

"I told you!" Bess exclaimed. "You *did* make a hit! Wish I had your technique!"

"Silly! Ned phoned me on a matter of business. This morning he found a ring near the hedge at the Raybolt grounds and he thought it might belong to me. It has a 'D' on it."

"That was just an excuse," Bess declared. "Of course, you didn't lose one."

"My guess is that the ring was lost by the man I saw running away from the fire. I can hardly wait to see it."

"And Ned, too," George added wickedly.

Nancy laughed at her friends' persistence, and was a bit surprised to find that she was blushing. A little farther on, the cousins said good-by and went to their separate homes. Luncheon was ready when Nancy reached hers. She ate with Hannah Gruen, who was very much interested in the ring Ned had found.

"Do you think it may be a clue?" she asked Nancy.

"Yes, to the writer of the diary. I'm going to study the little book thoroughly this afternoon and see if I can find a name beginning with 'D.'"

"But aren't you going to Mr. Peterson's?" Hannah asked.

"Later. I promised to be here for a phone call from the crippled children's home. I'm to help with their kiddie show next month. In the meantime, I think I'll call Mrs. Swenson to see how she and Honey are and if she has heard from her husband yet."

"Sorry," said the operator, when Nancy had dialed. "That number has been temporarily disconnected." Nancy surmised Mrs. Swenson had been forced to give up her telephone because of lack of funds.

"As soon as my car is repaired, I must drive to their house and see Honey and her mother," Nancy decided. "I only hope Mrs. Swenson will let me help."

Nancy spent the next few hours poring over the diary. But nowhere did she come across a name beginning with "D." She made one important discovery, however. At the bottom of a page written in Swedish, Nancy found a tiny ink drawing. She deduced that it was a diagram for some part of an electronic machine.

"I'll make no progress until I have Mr. Peterson translate this book for me," she thought.

Nancy was on the verge of going to the bakery by bus—but a glance at the clock told her the place would be closed. Besides, it was almost suppertime.

When Carson Drew arrived home, Nancy mentioned that her new friend, Ned Nickerson, was calling that evening.

"Oh, I see," her father drawled teasingly. "You want me to find it convenient to be away. Is that it?"

"Of course not. I particularly want you to meet Ned. He's bringing a ring that may interest you."

"Not a diamond, I hope!"

"Dad!" Nancy cried in exasperation. "You're as bad as Bess and George! Ned—Mr. Nickerson—is coming here on business."

"In that case," the lawyer said, his eyes twinkling, "I promise to be very proper and not embarrass you by asking the young man his intentions."

"You're absolutely hopeless!" Nancy laughed,

gave her father a hug, and ran into the kitchen.

Even though Ned's visit was to be one of "business," Nancy coaxed Hannah to bake a cake to be served with ice cream later in the evening.

Mrs. Gruen smiled knowingly, and immediately set to work. After supper, Nancy washed the dishes, then hurried upstairs. There was barely time for her to change into a flowered dress and high-heeled shoes before the doorbell rang. She hurried down to admit Ned.

The first greeting over, they were both a trifle embarrassed and felt a little shy. Nancy was glad that her father appeared just then, for the introduction relieved the situation.

She could tell that Mr. Drew liked Ned by the hearty way in which he shook hands. Many persons were awed in the presence of the attorney, but Nancy was delighted to discover that Ned felt at ease with him.

Seated in the comfortable living room, the lawyer skillfully directed the conversation. He had been rather curious concerning Nancy's new acquaintance. Mr. Drew sensed that his daughter was more interested in him than in other young men whom she dated.

"Tell us about the ring, Ned," Nancy urged. "May we see it?"

Ned took the object from his suit-coat pocket and handed it to her. Nancy observed that the signet ring probably belonged to a man, and was meant to be worn on the small finger. The polished black initial was set in relief on a gray background. Nancy studied the ring.

"It looks like an antique," she remarked, handing the ring to her father. "And the inscription inside *is* in Swedish, Dad. It's an expression my Swedish school friend always used: *Bär denna med tur*—wear this in luck!"

The discussion was interrupted at that moment by the ringing of the hall telephone. Carson Drew rose to answer it, and after a short conversation, came back and said regretfully to their guest:

"I must go down to the office—new development in a case—so I must excuse myself. Sorry. Glad to have met you, Ned."

After Mr. Drew had departed, Ned told Nancy the details of his call that morning at the Raybolt grounds. He had gone there before breakfast in order to view the wreckage before the arrival of curious townsfolk. The house had been razed by the fire. Nothing had been salvaged.

"Did the investigators find a clue to the cause of the fire?" Nancy asked.

"So far it's only a theory," Ned replied. "But I learned that the police and fire officials surmise explosives in the cellar may have been set off by remote control."

"But how? And by whom?" Nancy queried in amazement.

"They have no idea. Even a passing car with a

radio sending set could have done it accidentally."

"The house is pretty far from the road," Nancy countered. To herself she added, "Could that fleeing man who dropped the diary have used remote control—and not ever have been inside the house?"

Her thought was interrupted by Ned. "It's a queer case," he said. "Old Foxy Felix will get quite a jolt when he hears about the fire."

"Doesn't he know about it yet?" Nancy asked in surprise.

"Not according to latest reports. The Raybolts are still away. The neighbors tried to get in touch with them at the seashore hotel where they usually stay, but they're not registered."

"I wonder how much they will lose."

"Even with insurance, I'd say a goodly amount, including furniture and irreplaceable art objects."

"That will be a blow to the Raybolts, Ned."

"Yes, but everyone around Mapleton seems to think the old man had it coming to him. You hear all sorts of stories about the way he has connived to make money at other people's expense."

Nancy nodded, recalling what her father had told her. "I'm curious as to how Mr. Raybolt, especially, will take the loss."

"In the worst spirit, I imagine." Ned grinned. "If I find out, I'll let you know."

"I wish you would."

Nancy was tempted to tell Ned about the diary but decided not to until she knew more about it herself. After a very enjoyable evening, which ended with ice cream and Hannah's cake, Ned reluctantly stood up to depart.

"I don't know what to do with this ring," he said thoughtfully. "Why don't you keep it, Nancy?"

"I will if you want me to," she said eagerly. "Perhaps I'll find a clue to the owner through the inscription."

"That's what I figured. Let me know if you do." Ned grinned. "On second thought, perhaps I'd better drop over now and then to inquire."

Nancy's smile gave consent. Ned was still lingering on the porch steps when Carson Drew came up the walk. Nancy repeated what she had been told about the Raybolts' being unaware of their loss.

The lawyer raised his eyebrows in surprise. "Odd it's so hard to locate Raybolt. Perhaps, for the sake of my own client, I'll look into the matter."

"Why don't you, Dad? Mr. Raybolt may be able to furnish a clue to what caused the fire."

"You're right, Nancy," the lawyer said. "Raybolt may have had enemies who deliberately set fire to the house. If so, this might affect my case." The lawyer did not reveal why.

A few minutes later Ned said good night, jumped into his car, and drove away.

"How do you like him?" Nancy asked Mr. Drew hopefully as they walked into the house together.

"Nice boy," the lawyer commented. "I suppose I'll be seeing a lot of him from now on."

"Could be." Nancy laughed, kissed her father, and ran off to her room.

She did not retire immediately. Instead, she examined the signet ring more carefully. Finally she placed it in the bureau drawer with the diary.

"I have two clues now instead of one," Nancy assured herself jubilantly. "But the question is, are they connected?"

As she undressed, Nancy determined to call on the Swedish baker early the next morning.

"I *must* find out what the diary says!"

CHAPTER V

A Dangerous Detour

As soon as the morning's chores were finished, Nancy and Hannah Gruen set out on a bus for Oscar Peterson's bakery. Entering the clean little shop, fragrant with the odor of freshly baked bread, they were disappointed not to see the Swedish owner at the counter.

"Is Mr. Peterson in?" Nancy asked the girl in charge.

The young woman shook her head. "He's in bed upstairs, ill."

"Oh, I'm so sorry," said Nancy. "Give him our best wishes, and tell him we hope he'll be well soon."

"Oh, Mr. Peterson expects he'll feel good enough to come down to the shop this afternoon," the girl told her.

"Fine," Nancy replied. "I'll be back."

'After Mrs. Gruen had bought some rolls, she and Nancy left the shop with the diary still in Nancy's big purse.

Although disappointed, Nancy said, "Oh, well, I'll see Mr. Peterson later in the day."

Back home, Nancy again looked through the diary, hopeful of learning something from it. As she was puzzling over the blurred, cramped English, a word suddenly caught her eye.

"It's part of an address!" Nancy cried, highly elated. "I'm certain of it!"

Getting her father's magnifying glass from the desk, Nancy held it above the blurred writing, then read the words:

Riverwood Cottage, Sandy Creek.

Nancy stared at the address. "The Swensons!" she thought excitedly.

The young detective telephoned George and Bess and asked them to come over. When the cousins arrived, she rushed them into the living room and showed them the address.

"Riverwood Cottage, Sandy Creek!" Bess exclaimed. "That's where the Swensons live!"

"Boy, this certainly complicates matters," George declared.

Nancy nodded, knowing she had stumbled on a valuable, yet disturbing clue. Could it be that Honey's father was the man who had set fire to the Raybolt home? If so, what motive could he have had? Intuition warned Nancy that the clue might lead to heartbreak for Honey and her mother.

Nancy's face was so troubled that Bess and George begged her to tell them what she was thinking. Nancy revealed her concern for the Swensons, and also told about the ring Ned had left with her. She then pointed to the Sandy Creek notation.

"So far, this is the only clear-cut clue the diary has yielded." Nancy sighed. "But I hate to think what it may mean."

Bess and George nodded soberly.

"I can't imagine what Honey's father could have to do with the fire," Bess declared. "Yet everything fits in. The strange man you saw running away—the finding of the ring with the Swedish inscription near the hedge—"

"We don't know if it belongs to him," Nancy said quickly. "Remember, there's a 'D' on it, and his initials are J and S."

"Well, the *diary* must belong to Mr. Swenson, or someone who knows him," George said. "Otherwise, his address wouldn't be in it. I wonder what he's like."

"I wish we could meet him," Nancy returned gravely. She mentioned her futile phone call to the Swenson home.

"What are you going to do about the diary?" Bess questioned curiously. "Turn it over to the police?"

"No, I'll keep it until I can get a translation, and find out whether or not it means trouble for the Swensons."

"Of course this is all only circumstantial evidence," George reflected. "We're not certain the man you saw is Swedish. Although, according to your description, he could be."

"If he *is* Mr. Swenson, and he's guilty of setting the fire, I suppose he'll have to be brought to justice," Bess spoke up worriedly.

"I agree," Nancy said quietly. "But somehow I can't believe Honey's father would do a thing like that. She's such a sweet little thing, and her mother is a lovely person."

"I'd hate to get them involved, no matter what!" George declared feelingly. "I'm afraid they don't have enough to eat as it is, and if the father should go to prison—"

"Let's try to take an optimistic view," Nancy said. "Perhaps neither the diary nor the ring is Mr. Swenson's, or if they are, he may have a perfectly blameless reason for having been on the Raybolt grounds."

"I think you're right about working this puzzle out by yourself, Nancy," George commented. "You've had wonderful success on other mysteries. This may be your chance to help Honey and her mother."

"I wish my car were ready now!"

"When will it be?" Bess asked.

"Not until later today. I'll tell you what! Let's walk to the garage. It won't do any harm to spur the mechanic on a bit. When we come back we can stop at Dad's office and ask him if he has traced the Raybolts. He promised to try."

At the garage, the girls were dismayed to learn that repairs on the convertible were only half finished. The mechanic, however, assured Nancy that the car would be ready by midafternoon.

The girls stopped a few minutes at a department store where Bess bought some kitchen spoons for her mother, then they continued to Carson Drew's office. As usual, the lawyer was busy, but he found time to chat with his daughter and her friends.

"I had my secretary try to get in touch with Mr. Raybolt," he told Nancy, "but so far she hasn't been able to locate him—or his wife. They seem to have vanished!"

"Maybe Felix Raybolt has gone into hiding," Nancy suggested with a wry smile.

"Oh, I've no doubt he'll be heard from, once the news reaches him that his house has been ruined," said Mr. Drew. "I'll keep trying to locate him."

It was nearly twelve o'clock when the girls left the lawyer's office. Bess and George said they must go home to luncheon.

"Come have a bite with me," Nancy urged.

"Then we can all go to see Mr. Peterson—if you don't mind taking the bus."

George and Bess eagerly accepted the invitation. They were as curious as Nancy concerning the contents of the diary. Hannah Gruen served a delicious meal, and it was nearly three o'clock before the girls finally boarded a bus to call on the Swedish baker.

"I'm dying to know what the diary says," George declared enthusiastically.

"I hope it won't make things look any worse for Honey's father," Bess murmured apprehensively.

As they alighted near the bakery, the girls were distressed to see an ambulance parked directly in front of the shop. A small group of spectators had gathered.

"There's been an accident!" Nancy exclaimed, quickening her step. "Oh, I hope nothing has happened to dear old Oscar Peterson!"

The girls reached the bakery at the same moment that the ambulance drove away, siren wailing.

"What happened?" Nancy asked a woman who was standing near the door of the shop. "Was someone hurt?"

"It was Mr. Peterson. He had a relapse, and the doctor ordered him to the hospital. Expect he'll be there a few days."

"How dreadful!" said Bess. "But, Nancy, what will you do about the diary now?"

Nancy, mainly concerned about the kindly baker, did not answer immediately. Finally she suggested they ask the baker's assistant if she knew of anyone who understood Swedish.

The woman gladly called several people, but none were at home. Nancy even phoned her father to see if he could recommend someone. But Mr. Drew was not at his office.

The girls were a little discouraged, but Nancy said, "We can still work on the mystery. My car should be finished by this time. If it is, we can drive over and visit Honey and her mother."

"That's a swell idea!" Bess and George chorused.

When they reached the garage, the girls were overjoyed to find the convertible ready. "Looks almost as good as new!" Nancy said, pleased. "I'll write a check for the amount."

To her chagrin, she had forgotten her checkbook.

"That's all right," the mechanic said. "I'm very busy, anyhow. I'll make out the bill later and drop it off at your home."

"Fine," Nancy said with a smile. Then she and the cousins phoned their homes from an outside booth to report their destination. A few minutes later they set off on the highway for Sandy Creek.

Nancy slowed as she drove past the Raybolt estate. The girls glanced at the charred ruins of the once-beautiful mansion.

"I wish we had time to stop and talk to the men investigating the cause of the fire," Nancy said. "But we'd better get to the Swensons' first."

About ten miles farther on, Nancy came to a sawhorse across the road. "Detour!" George groaned. "It must've been put up yesterday."

"It isn't very long," Bess declared optimistically. "I can see the end of it."

The road had been closed to permit the construction of a new steel bridge. The bypass wound down into a valley, crossing the Muskoka River a quarter of a mile south.

"We'll lose time on this dirt road," Nancy remarked, turning into the detour. "Poor car! It'll be lucky to get through without jolting to pieces."

The road was ungraded and recent rains had left it rutty. In addition, it was narrow, with hardly any places wide enough for two cars to pass. Even though Nancy drove slowly, the ride was a bumpy one.

"Good way to break a spring—on a road like this!" she declared.

"Or a bone!" Bess added wryly.

A moment later the girls became aware of a loud, insistent honking behind them.

"Big truck right in back of you, Nancy," George observed.

"I know. Well, the driver will just have to wait. *He* can't pass me on this narrow stretch."

But the blowing of the truck's horn continued until Nancy became irritated, then indignant.

"What *is* the matter with that man?"

Nancy increased her speed, hoping to leave the impatient driver behind. But he speeded up, keeping close to the convertible. *Honk! Honk! Honk!*

"If he doesn't s-stop that, I'll s-scream!" Bess complained. "And if we g-go any faster, I'll l-lose all my teeth."

The convertible was now bumping up and down unmercifully. George turned

around in her seat to glare at the horn-blowing driver. "Don't give him an inch!" she told Nancy.

"Wouldn't do him any good if I did. His truck's too big to pass, and I'm certainly not going into a

ditch to let him get by! He'll have to wait until we reach the end of this detour!"

"What's his big hurry, anyhow?" George grumbled. "Probably just trying to make us nervous."

"Well, he's certainly succeeding so far as I'm concerned," Bess said.

Just then the girls came within sight of a wooden bridge—the end of the torturous road.

"Thank goodness!" Bess cried.

With the truck still bearing down on the convertible, Nancy drove onto the bridge.

"It doesn't look very safe," Bess remarked uneasily. "No wonder they're building a new bridge."

"It doesn't sound safe, either!" George cried out as the loose planks creaked alarmingly under the weight of the car. "If that truck tries to pass us, we'll all crash through!"

But at that moment the girls heard the heavy truck clatter onto the wooden planks. "He's crazy!" George exclaimed. "This bridge will never hold us both!"

The words were barely out of her mouth when there came a cracking, splintering sound.

"Nancy!" Bess shrieked. "Look out!"

CHAPTER VI

Nancy's Strategy

AT BESS's warning, Nancy glanced at the rear-view mirror and saw that the driver of the heavy truck did indeed intend to pass her! There was only one way for her to avert an accident: take her car full speed ahead.

"Here goes!" she cried out, and the convertible shot forward.

The three girls held their breaths, praying that the bridge would be strong enough to hold both vehicles. The old bridge creaked and groaned but held up despite a plank cracked by the truck.

Nancy had barely reached the far end when the truck sped past her at an alarming rate. It grazed her car and tore off part of the bridge railing. The driver rushed on pell-mell.

"That fellow's a madman!" George exclaimed angrily. "He should be arrested for reckless driving!"

"I wish I had taken his license number so we could report him to the police!" Bess added.

Nancy sighed. "At this point I'm just glad my car doesn't have to go into the repair shop again! I have a lot of work to do trying to solve the mystery of the Raybolt fire."

As the girls drove on toward Sandy Creek, they finally forgot their indignation. When they reached the town, Nancy asked a policeman for directions. Following these, she arrived at a section near the river where small houses were crowded together. Bess and George carefully scanned the weather-worn cottages, searching for one with the name "Riverwood."

Bess caught sight of it first. "I see Honey out front!" she said eagerly. "Look! Isn't she sweet?"

As Nancy halted the car before the old house, she saw that the child had fallen asleep under a tree. A large dog lay at her feet as though on guard. At the girls' approach he jumped up and growled.

Nancy and her friends scarcely knew whether to advance or retreat, for the dog looked vicious and seemed determined to protect his tiny charge from the strangers. As they were hesitating, the child awoke. She recognized the girls at once, and scrambling up from the grass, ran toward them.

Despite her faded play suit and badly scuffed shoes, Honey was an attractive youngster. Her real name was Helen Ebba Swenson, but she had always been called Honey because of her sweet disposition. Her eyes were a bright blue, her fair skin was dotted with brown freckles, and her golden hair curled in a hundred ringlets.

"Hello, Honey," Nancy greeted her. "Is your mother at home?"

The child shook her head. "Mommy's gone to the post office to get a letter from Daddy. I wanted to go, but she said it was too far for me to walk."

"Isn't your father at home?" Nancy inquired softly.

"Oh, no," Honey replied in her most grown-up manner. "He's been gone a long time. Mommy's worried. That's why she went to the post office today."

Nancy and her friends exchanged quick glances. Mrs. Swenson apparently still was awaiting word from her husband.

"Mommy'll be coming home soon," Honey went on, " 'cause it's suppertime. I'm hungry, too."

With a pang Nancy saw that the youngster looked thinner than ever.

"Mommy said if she could sell some of the eggs from our hens, she'd bring me something good to eat. I'm tired of eggs. We eat them all the time since Daddy left."

"Haven't you anything else?" George asked bluntly.

"We have a little bread. Mommy says we must make our money last until we hear from Daddy. She doesn't know where he went and she cries a lot."

Honey went on to tell the girls about her dog, Hans. "Daddy and I used to take him walking. Hans misses Daddy same as I do. Nancy, let's all go in the house. I want to show you my toys Daddy made."

Honey led the way inside. The living room was neat and smelled fresh and clean. There was little furniture, one very small rug, and no draperies at the windows. Nancy's eye was attracted to a photograph that stood on a small table.

"Whose picture is that?" she asked Honey.

"My daddy!" Honey answered proudly.

Nancy's heart sank. It was a photograph of the stranger she had seen running away from the fire!

"Oh, dear!" she thought. "This is the worst situation I've ever been in!"

By this time Honey had brought out her toys from a cupboard. All were homemade, and several were mechanical, each one cleverly fashioned.

"My daddy's an in-ven-tor." The little girl had trouble pronouncing the word. "That's why he went away—to get back one of his in-ven-tions."

Nancy, Bess, and George looked at one another horrified. The same thoughts raced through their minds. Mr. Swenson an inventor! The Swedish

diary Nancy had found at the scene of the fire!
Mr. Raybolt's broken promises to inventors!

Bess, to hide tears that were gathering, walked
into the kitchen. On impulse she opened the re-
frigerator and cupboards. They were practically
empty. She came back and whispered to the
others.

"Something must be done," Bess declared.
"Why, Honey and her mother haven't enough to
keep them from starving."

"It's up to us," Nancy announced firmly. "I
have an idea! We'll all eat supper here!"

As George and Bess looked puzzled, Nancy
hastily explained her plan. She would drive to
Sandy Creek, pick up Honey's mother, and purchase enough food for supper.

"We'll have a regular feast," she promised.
"How much money do you girls have with you?"

"Two dollars and ten cents," Bess said, opening
her purse.

"I have only one dollar with me," George announced apologetically.

"With what I have that will be enough," Nancy
said briskly. "I'll pay you both back when we get
home."

"No you won't," George protested. "We're all
in on this."

"Fine!" Nancy smiled. "You girls stay here
with Honey. I'll hurry back as quickly as I can."

"Honey's mother may not like our interfering," Bess ventured doubtfully.

"I'll be tactful," Nancy promised.

Honey followed her to the car, eying Nancy with worshipful eyes.

"I like ice cream," she ventured with a timid smile.

"I'll bring some," Nancy said. "And plenty of other good things. A bone, with meat on it, for Hans, too!"

She drove away swiftly. A quarter mile down the road she caught sight of a woman trudging along dejectedly. Honey's mother!

Nancy was quick to observe the downcast expression on the woman's face and guessed that she had received no word from her husband. Undoubtedly Mrs. Swenson had hoped that he would send money so that she might purchase food.

"Poor thing!" Nancy thought. "I don't believe I can ever bring myself to tell her about the diary. If her husband has done wrong, it will break her heart."

Pulling over to the side of the road, she called a cheery greeting. Mrs. Swenson started in surprise as she recognized Nancy.

"Won't you let me drive you home?" Nancy asked her.

"But you're going in the opposite direction," Mrs. Swenson protested.

"Oh, that's perfectly all right," Nancy replied, as the woman wearily climbed in beside her.

"I'm on my way to town to buy some things," Nancy explained, "but as soon as I've purchased them, I'll take you straight home. You won't mind the extra ride, will you?"

"Indeed I won't." Mrs. Swenson smiled faintly. "I don't feel as though I could walk another step. I must get home soon, though, for my little girl hasn't had her supper."

Nancy wondered what would be the best way in which to broach the plan to Mrs. Swenson about the "feast."

"Well, here goes!" Nancy thought. "If she refuses, there's nothing the girls and I can do except return home."

CHAPTER VII

A Disclosure

AFTER outlining her plan for the supper party, Nancy waited expectantly for Mrs. Swenson's response. During the moment of silence, she clearly read the woman's thoughts. She was battling with her pride.

"How kind of you to take an interest in us!" Mrs. Swenson said at last. "I appreciate it more than I can tell you."

"Then I may go ahead with my shopping?" Nancy asked eagerly.

"Yes, it will be wonderful to have a 'feast,' as you call it. We haven't had one since my husband left." Mrs. Swenson caught herself quickly, and said, "Joe is away looking for work. I'm sure he'll send me money in a few days and then I can repay you for—"

"Oh, but this is a special party," Nancy interrupted gaily. "You mustn't think of repaying me."

During the ride to town, Mrs. Swenson seldom spoke. She leaned wearily against the cushion, a half-smile playing over her pale face. Her weary blue eyes were kind, but the privations brought on by poverty and worry had stamped grim lines about her mouth.

Nancy parked the convertible on the main street of Sandy Creek and insisted that Mrs. Swenson assist her in selecting the food for the feast. They chose a quantity of staples, then Nancy added as many luxuries as she could afford —ice cream, a thick juicy steak, fresh fruit and vegetables, cake and an assortment of melons.

"You're buying enough to last a week!" Mrs. Swenson declared.

That was exactly what Nancy had intended to do. Not until she had practically exhausted her funds would she listen to the other's protests.

"If it weren't for Honey, I never would permit you to spend money on us," Mrs. Swenson said as they climbed into the car. "We're not accustomed to accepting charity. When my husband was employed, we lived well. We should still be well off if he hadn't been cheated out of his rights!"

This gave Nancy an opening, and as they drove back toward Riverwood Cottage she diplomatically questioned the woman. Mrs. Swenson, however, revealed very little about her husband. She seemed eager to impress Nancy with his kindness, rather than his apparent irresponsibility.

"Joe has always been good to me and he adores Honey. Some folks say he's lazy, but that isn't true. He's always worked—harder than most folks. He's an inventor, and if he hadn't been cheated out of his patents, we'd be wealthy—"

She broke off as the convertible turned a corner and a voice called out, "Hi, Nancy!"

"Ned Nickerson!" she exclaimed, and pulled to the curb behind Ned's parked car.

With a pleased grin which spread over his entire face, Ned jumped from behind the wheel and came hurrying toward the convertible.

"What are you doing here?" he asked.

"Oh, just prowling about." Nancy laughed. She introduced Mrs. Swenson, then said, "What are *you* doing in Sandy Creek?"

"On an errand for my mother. I'm about to rush home for something to eat. I'm nearly starved."

"Better come with us," Nancy proposed impetuously. "We're having a feast at Mrs. Swenson's."

Ned accepted the invitation without an instant's hesitation, and promised to follow in his car as soon as he had phoned home.

It was only a short distance to the cottage, and Mrs. Swenson showed no inclination to resume the interrupted conversation. Nancy had hoped that she would tell more about her husband's work, but the woman did not volunteer any additional information.

"I'll talk to Mrs. Swenson about it before I leave the cottage," Nancy promised herself. "I must get to the bottom of the mystery."

The few hints that Mrs. Swenson had dropped only served to trouble Nancy further. Since Joe Swenson was an inventor, it seemed reasonable that he had gone to Mr. Raybolt to retrieve something of his. If no one were home, he might have become a housebreaker, then an arsonist. Nancy suddenly chided herself.

"I mustn't have such thoughts! Time enough to draw conclusions when I've heard Mr. Swenson's side of the story! Right now, I'll say nothing to ruin our little party."

As Nancy parked in front of Riverwood Cottage, Bess, George, and Honey came running to see what she had brought. The little girl squealed with delight as she peered into the various packages.

"You didn't forget Hans's bone?" she asked.

"I should say not," Nancy told her. "The butcher gave us the best one he had."

Ned arrived, and everyone helped carry in the bundles. As Nancy stepped into the cottage it was her turn to be surprised. During her absence the girls had decorated the living-dining room with flowers from the garden and had brought out the best china, a lovely set of delftware.

"What beautiful dishes!" Nancy exclaimed admiringly.

"They're all I have left of our good possessions," Mrs. Swenson said. "The set was given to me as a wedding present. I must sell the dishes soon, but I keep putting it off."

"It seems a shame to sell a wedding gift," Bess remarked sympathetically. "Especially such a lovely one as this."

Under the influence of the young people, Mrs. Swenson brightened. It was impossible to be downhearted around Ned and Nancy, who kept up a constant stream of good-natured banter. Mrs. Swenson, an excellent cook, took charge of preparing the meal, but she had four able assistants. Honey and Hans hovered near the stove where the steak was sizzling.

"Hans has his canine eye on another bone!" Ned laughed. "Well, he won't get it until we've picked it bare."

Nancy had not misnamed the supper, for it really was a feast. There was plenty of everything and it was a pleasure to see Honey's eyes grow big at the sight of each steaming dish that was brought to the table.

It was a happy meal, and Ned proved to be a very interesting dinner companion. Even Mrs.

Swenson's sober face lighted up and she ate her food with enjoyment. Nancy entered into the lighthearted conversation, but her mind was far from carefree. Several times during the meal George gazed at her significantly as though to ask what she intended to do about the diary. The girls had come to Sandy Creek to learn certain facts, but now that they realized how affairs were at the Swenson cottage, it seemed unkind to bring further trouble upon the family.

"I want to show you my little baby chicks," Honey announced when the meal was over. "I have ten yellow ones—all my own."

Ned, Bess, and George obligingly followed the child outside.

"Coming?" Bess asked Nancy.

"No, I'll stay and help with the dishes."

Nancy felt that it was her opportunity to talk with Mrs. Swenson alone. Yet, after the others had gone, she did not know how to launch the important subject. As she scraped the dishes, she cautiously broached the subject of nationalities.

"We're Swedish," Mrs. Swenson declared. "You probably guessed that."

Nancy had, but her heart sank at the definite assertion.

"You speak perfect English," she replied.

"My husband is a university man," the woman returned proudly. "He has always corrected my English and helped me with it."

"What were the other names in your families?" Nancy asked, smiling.

"My maiden name was the same as that of Joe's mother—Dahl." Nancy stifled a gasp. The ring with the initial "D" must have been inherited by Joe Swenson! Now she *must* find out about the diary!

"I've often heard that people who move to this country keep diaries. Did your family follow the custom?" Nancy inquired, trying to make her question sound uninquisitive.

"The Swensons always did, even at home. My husband kept a diary in which he also told of his inventions. He hoped that this would help keep his ideas safe. But—" Mrs. Swenson stopped speaking and gazed into space.

Nancy pretended not to notice the long pause. Finally she asked, "Did your husband always carry the diary with him?"

"Yes, he did."

At this affirmation of her suspicions, Nancy almost dropped a plate. She quickly caught it, but thought, "Evidence is piling up against Joe Swenson at an alarming rate!"

Presently Mrs. Swenson spoke again. "Nancy, I can't understand why I haven't heard from my husband," she confided. "Joe has been gone a month. He was sure of finding work and promised to send money home. But I haven't had a single letter from him. That's the reason I went to the post office today. But there was no mail for me. Oh, Nancy, I'm so worried about Joe. Something may have happened to him!"

"Oh, I don't think so," Nancy said quickly.

Mrs. Swenson grabbed the girl's arm. "Why do you say that?" she cried out. "Do you know something about Joe?"

Nancy was dumfounded. What was she going to say now?

CHAPTER VIII

Worried Sleuths

Taking a deep breath, Nancy put an arm around Mrs. Swenson. "I'm sure your husband carried identification. If anything had happened to him, surely you would have been notified by this time."

"But what about his not writing to me?" Mrs. Swenson persisted. "It's unlike Joe not to keep a promise."

"Well, that puzzles me too," Nancy confessed. "But I'm sure you'll hear from him soon."

"Oh, I hope so. It should have been easy for Joe to find work, because he's very skillful. But as I told you before, he was cheated out of a fair deal on his cleverest invention. Unfortunately, he entrusted the drawings to an unscrupulous man who promised to take out patents for him—but didn't!"

"How dreadful!" Nancy remarked.

"Yes, the man took the patents out under his own name. He deliberately stole them from Joe."

"Who is the man?" Nancy asked tensely, yet fearing the answer.

Mrs. Swenson hesitated an instant and then said, "Perhaps I shouldn't give his name, but since you'll most likely never see him, it can do no harm. The man who cheated Joe, who broke his spirit, is Felix Raybolt!"

"Felix Raybolt!" Nancy echoed.

She had expected this answer, yet hearing the name gave her a distinct shock.

"Yes," Mrs. Swenson returned, looking curiously at the girl. "Do you know him?"

"Only by reputation," Nancy answered. "I did hear that his house burned."

This was news to Mrs. Swenson. "Was anyone hurt?" she asked.

"The police and firemen think the house was unoccupied at the time."

At that moment Honey and her new friends came in from the garden.

"Nancy," Bess said, "don't you think we'd better start for home? The sun is setting and we ought to cross that shaky bridge before dark."

"Yes," Nancy agreed. "We'll leave right away."

While the other girls were gathering their handbags and saying good-by, she found an opportunity to speak to Ned privately.

"Have you heard any news about the Ray-bolts?" she asked in a low tone.

"Not a word. They haven't been located yet."

Nancy now hurriedly explained that she believed she had found the owner of the ring—Mr. Swenson.

Ned frowned. "This may involve him as a suspect in the fire. What a shame! Mrs. Swenson and Honey are such nice people. I like that little girl a lot."

"So do I," Nancy admitted. "I wish I could do something for them—mainly, prove Joe Swenson's innocent."

"I think you've done a lot already. It's my turn now. Do you suppose they'd be offended if I left five dollars?"

"It would be a blessing, Ned. I don't believe they have a penny in the house. Why not hide it somewhere?"

"That's a good idea," Ned said. "Mrs. Swenson can't very well protest if she doesn't find it until after we're gone!"

Without being detected, Ned managed to slip one corner of the five-dollar bill under the vase of flowers on the table. Then they said good-by, promising to return for another visit.

Nancy had told Ned about the broken-down bridge, and the young man insisted upon accompanying the girls past the detour. They found

that the smashed railing had been marked by
warning lights. As soon as Nancy had crossed over
in safety, Ned waved and drove on ahead.

"He certainly intends to look after you,
Nancy," Bess teased mischievously. "Honestly, he
has a terrible case!"

"Hush!" Nancy retorted, but she was not dis-
pleased.

As they rode toward River Heights, she told
the girls of her talk with Mrs. Swenson.

"Things are beginning to look black for her
husband," Bess declared. "He certainly had a
motive if Mr. Raybolt stole the patent to his invention."

"All the evidence points that way," Nancy admitted, "and yet I can't believe he's guilty."

"He'll be sent to jail if he is," George stated
flatly. "What do you intend to do?"

"I don't know." Nancy sighed deeply. "I was
never in such a quandary in my life! If he goes to
prison, Mrs. Swenson and Honey will be without
means of support—to say nothing of the family
name being clouded."

"But it isn't right to protect a criminal," Bess
insisted.

"He's innocent until proved otherwise," Nancy
reminded her friend. "Before doing anything
more, I'm going to have a long talk with Dad."

By the time the girls arrived in River Heights,

darkness had fallen. Nancy dropped her friends at their homes. When she reached her own house, she found Hannah tidying the kitchen.

"Isn't Dad home yet?" Nancy asked.

"No, he telephoned he wouldn't be back until late tonight."

Nancy was disappointed that her father had not returned. It was only a little after eight o'clock, but after talking to the housekeeper a few minutes, Nancy went to her bedroom.

"I'll have another look at that diary," she thought. "Perhaps I'll be able to make something out of it, now that I know more about Joe Swenson."

For one hour Nancy, with added incentive, patiently applied herself to the task of deciphering the cramped English scrawl. She looked at the drawing again and wondered whether it was a sketch for part of the stolen invention. Finally she was able to distinguish a few paragraphs— mostly notations of supplies purchased from various manufacturing concerns.

"Maybe Joe Swenson found a job in one of those places!" Nancy thought optimistically. "I'll go from one to another and inquire!"

Any possible lead was welcome at this point, Nancy told herself excitedly. She scanned the notations again. Her eyes lingered on the name of a company in the small city of Stanford.

"That's where Mr. Baylor Weston lives—the

man who ran into my car," the young detective murmured. "I'll go to Stanford first, and see Mr. Weston at the same time!"

When Nancy came down to breakfast the next morning she found a sealed envelope beside her plate. She was mystified to note there was no return address on it.

"A man left the envelope early this morning," Mrs. Gruen told Nancy.

CHAPTER IX

A Scare

EAGERLY Nancy tore open the envelope and unfolded the sheet inside.

"A bill for the repairs to my car," she told Hannah Gruen. "It sounds very fair. Mr. Baylor Weston—who ran into me—shouldn't mind paying this amount."

The housekeeper laughed. "The garage mechanic was certainly prompt in delivering his bill."

"I asked him to be," Nancy defended the man. "I want to present this bill and the Mapleton garage one right away to Mr. Weston."

"That's the spirit," came a voice from the doorway. "Good morning!" Mr. Drew walked in, kissed Nancy, and asked, "How are you, Hannah?"

Carson Drew took his place at the head of the table, then said, "Nancy, I learned yesterday that

Baylor Weston owns an electronics factory in Stanford."

"What a break for me!" Nancy exclaimed. "I can do two errands at once." She told about having seen the name of the Stanford Electronics Company in the diary, and her intention of finding out if Mr. Swenson worked there.

"Excellent idea," said Mr. Drew. "And now for more news."

"You found Mr. Raybolt?" Nancy asked eagerly.

"Yes and no. To be strictly correct, I found *Mrs.* Raybolt."

"Where is she, Dad?"

"At a summer resort on Lake Mentor. I talked with Mrs. Raybolt on the phone. She became very upset about the fire and told me she would return today to look into the matter."

"And her husband?"

"She didn't say where he is and was rather evasive when I questioned her about him."

"I'd like to talk to Mrs. Raybolt, Dad."

"Well, why don't you? She'll surely stay at the Maplecroft Inn because it's the only hotel within three miles of the Raybolt estate. My guess is that if you go there for luncheon you might meet her."

"That's a grand idea!" Nancy said excitedly. "I see now why you're called River Heights' leading lawyer!"

She asked her father if he knew of someone who could translate the diary. "I've already checked," Mr. Drew replied. "But my two friends who speak Swedish are away on vacation."

Nancy was so enthusiastic about the idea of visiting the inn that as soon as she had finished breakfast, she phoned Bess and George. Always eager for adventure, they quickly said they would love to go along. By eleven o'clock the three girls were en route.

"I have a feeling that we're about to learn something important!" Nancy confided to her friends.

It was only a few minutes after twelve when the girls reached the pleasant little inn. Nancy parked beside a row of cars at the rear of the building. The girls went inside and inquired for Mrs. Raybolt.

"She hasn't arrived yet," the desk clerk said, "but we expect her any minute."

The girls strolled outside and sat down on the porch. But after an hour had elapsed, the wealthy woman still had not arrived. Bess gave a huge sigh. "I'm starved! We may as well have luncheon. I don't believe Mrs. Raybolt is coming."

"It looks that way," Nancy admitted in disappointment. "Wait a second, though, here comes another car."

Hopefully, the girls watched as a large automobile swept up the driveway. A chauffeur assisted a frail, nervous-looking woman of middle age to alight. She clung unsteadily to his arm and for a moment the girls thought she would faint.

The chauffeur said encouragingly, "You'll feel better, Mrs. Raybolt, after you have had your lunch."

So *this* was Mrs. Raybolt! She made no response other than to give a low moan. Still leaning on the chauffeur's arm, she walked uncertainly up the porch steps.

"Goodness," Bess exclaimed in a whisper, "isn't that poor woman pale? She looks ill. I'm surprised her husband left her alone."

Nancy did not comment. She was watching Mrs. Raybolt closely and it struck her that the woman *was* actually ill. As she reached the porch, Mrs. Raybolt caught hold of a post for support.

"I can't go on," she whispered weakly. Then she fainted.

The chauffeur caught her in his arms as she fell and eased her to the level of the porch. Nancy and her friends, thoroughly alarmed, rushed forward to be of assistance.

"I'll get some water!" Nancy cried, and dashed inside. The desk clerk came rushing out.

"Take her into the manager's office," he suggested kindly. "I'll call a doctor."

The chauffeur quickly explained that they had just been to the scene of the fire. Then Mrs. Raybolt was carried inside and made comfortable on the couch. Her face was pale, but as Nancy applied a wet cloth to her forehead, she revived somewhat.

"Felix!" she moaned. "Oh, Felix!"

"Your husband will be here soon," Nancy assured her soothingly.

Her words had an astounding effect upon the woman. She half raised herself and her eyes, fluttering open, had a wild expression in them.

"My husband is dead," she moaned. "He burned to death."

"She must be hysterical," said the manager's secretary. "I hope the doctor gets here soon."

"Your husband isn't dead," Nancy said comfortingly.

Mrs. Raybolt appeared not to hear the girl, for she went on wildly, "He burned to death in the fire! Oh, Felix!"

"What's she talking about?" demanded the manager, who had just entered the room.

"I'm sure her husband wasn't in the house at the time it burned," said Nancy. "The investigators found no evidence of anyone having been trapped inside."

Yet, as she spoke, doubt besieged Nancy. How did she know that Felix Raybolt had not been trapped inside the house? True, no body had been found, but what if the explosion— Nancy put the horrible thought out of her mind.

Mrs. Raybolt revived sufficiently to sit up, and

"I can't go on!" the woman whispered weakly

after she had drunk the glass of water Nancy handed her, she appeared to be less agitated.

"You must be mistaken about your husband," Bess told her gently.

"No! No!" the woman cried. "He went there the night of the fire to see a man on business. I had a feeling he shouldn't go and I tried to stop him, but he wouldn't listen to me. I haven't heard from Felix since that night."

Mrs. Raybolt broke down and sobbed hysterically. Nancy asked the name of the man whom Felix Raybolt had gone to see.

"I don't know," she replied. "Felix never confided any business matters to me. He resented questions. I do know that Felix was uneasy about the appointment."

"Why?"

"He anticipated possible physical violence."

Nancy and her friends gulped. If the person with whom Mr. Raybolt had an appointment was Joe Swenson, here was still another count against the Swedish inventor.

At that moment the doctor appeared. He briskly cleared the room, insisting that the patient have absolute quiet. Nancy and her friends left with the others.

"Well, what do you think of the case now?" George whispered tensely.

"I think," Nancy returned soberly, "that things look very black for poor Joe Swenson."

The three girls ate luncheon in silence. They did not want to discuss the mystery in public, and were too concerned to talk of anything else.

When they finished eating, Nancy stopped at the reservation desk and asked the clerk for directions to Stanford. "Take the short cut across Sunview Mountain," he advised. "It's half the distance it would be by the main road."

Nancy thanked him and the girls went to the car. As they were about to drive off, a state trooper stopped Nancy and said, "A word of advice, young ladies. We believe a dangerous criminal is hiding in the vicinity. Keep your doors locked."

"What did he do?" Bess asked fearfully.

"It's suspected he's a firebug, a robber, and—well, he may use a gun on anyone who gets in his way."

"What's his name?" Nancy inquired, her heart sinking in the fear that it would be Joe Swenson.

To her relief, the officer replied that the police were still working to establish the man's identity. "But watch your step, and if you should see anything suspicious, be sure to report it to us."

"I will," Nancy promised, and drove off.

Five miles farther on she turned into the narrow short cut across Sunview Mountain. The twisting road, bordered by tangled undergrowth and dense woods, was deserted.

Bess shivered. "The wildest section in the

county!" she exclaimed nervously. "Just the sort of place a criminal would choose for a hideout. For goodness sake, Nancy, step on the gas!"

"This *is* a spooky road," George murmured presently. "Wouldn't it be funny if we should come upon Joe Swenson, peering out at us from the bushes?"

"Funny?" Bess demanded. "I'd be frightened out of my wits. Wouldn't you, Nancy?"

"Well, I don't know," the other returned truthfully. "I'm eager to find that man."

"So am I," Bess replied, "but I'd rather not run into any stranger in this out-of-the-way spot!"

Nancy did not reply immediately, and her friends noticed that she appeared to be scanning the woods searchingly.

"You think the criminal actually might be hiding along this road?" Bess demanded anxiously.

Nancy nodded. "It's possible."

"Turn back!" Bess pleaded. "No telling what he might do to us!"

"Don't get jittery," Nancy advised. "Remember, we *have* to find out if Joe Swenson works at the plant in Stanford."

As they drove along the winding road, the three girls maintained a vigilant lookout. Suddenly Bess cried out:

"There's a man ahead, at the side of the road! He's motioning us to stop! Don't do it, Nancy!"

CHAPTER X

A Spooky Shack

INSTINCTIVELY Nancy pressed down hard on the gas pedal and shot past the man. In the rear-view mirror she saw an astonished look on his face. She slowed to a normal pace and laughed in relief.

"A hitchhiker! He probably thinks I'm crazy!"

The stranger did not in the least resemble a criminal type. He looked kind and pleasant.

"Better safe then sorry," Bess defended herself as they left the amazed hitchhiker far behind.

"I'll have to agree with you on that," said George.

Presently Nancy came to a fork in the road and stopped the convertible. There were no signs to indicate which road led toward the Weston factory.

"I'd turn to the left," Bess advised.

"The right-hand turn looks more likely to me," George insisted. "Look—I see a shack over among those trees. Why not inquire there?"

"A good idea!" Nancy approved. She pulled up before the shack and flung open the car door. George did the same and promptly stepped out.

But Bess held back. "No telling *who* lives there, girls! M-maybe that criminal!"

"George and I will go," said Nancy. "You stay here, Bess."

"Not on your life. If you're going, I'll go, too."

George and Nancy were already pushing their way through the brush, and Bess, fearful of being left alone, hurried after them. The shack was located in a tiny clearing which was enclosed on three sides by dense forest.

The girls were halfway to the cabin when Bess clutched Nancy's arm. "There's someone in the bushes—over by the grape arbor—watching us!"

The three girls huddled together, afraid to continue. They could see the motionless figure peeping out at them.

Suddenly Nancy burst into laughter.

"A scarecrow!" she exclaimed. "Bess, this makes the second time you've given us a scare!"

Bess looked sheepish and made no response.

"Come on!" George said in disgust. "We're acting like babies!"

The girls approached the shack with a boldness they did not feel. Bess remarked nervously that the place seemed unnaturally quiet.

Summoning her courage, Nancy knocked on the door. There was no response. She knocked again, louder than before.

"I heard someone moving!" George whispered tensely.

Nancy thought she had heard something. A little chill of excitement ran down her spine. Was someone hiding inside?

"Let's go back!" Bess urged fearfully.

"One more try," Nancy begged, and knocked again.

When no answer came, Nancy gently turned the knob. The door opened so quickly she almost plunged headlong into the one-room shack. She sprang back, expecting to face an occupant. The room was empty. The few furnishings were broken down and covered with dust.

"Another joke on us!" Nancy said. "I'd have sworn I heard someone moving in here!"

"So would I," murmured Bess in a relieved tone. "What a creepy place!"

The girls tiptoed around the shack, side-stepping the dirt, and ducking their heads, as they avoided the heavy cobwebs.

"Nobody home!" announced Nancy, gaily shaking off her former apprehensive mood.

"No one has used this shack in months," George declared.

"We may as well run along," said Nancy.

Returning to their car, the girls agreed after some debate to take the right-hand fork. A few minutes' driving took them to the foot of Sunview Mountain.

"I see a town ahead," Nancy observed. "We'll stop there and inquire if we're on the right road."

When they reached the main section of the village, Nancy managed to attract the attention of a policeman, who left his post and came over to the car.

"The road to the Weston factory?" he repeated. "You should have taken the left fork several miles back."

The girls exchanged looks of consternation. After their recent experiences the thought of returning over the same route was cheerless indeed.

"There's another way you can get there," the policeman told them, "but it will take you a little longer."

"That's all right," Nancy said thankfully.

He then explained in detail how they could reach the factory. Nancy thanked him and drove on.

"We'll have to hurry," she remarked to her friends, "or the factory will be closed. Just our luck to take the wrong turn."

Swift driving partially made up for lost time, but Nancy's wrist watch warned her that it was nearly four o'clock when they at last reached the factory on the outskirts of Stanford. It took the girls a few minutes to locate the office.

Nancy presented herself to the young woman in charge, stating that she wished to see Mr. Baylor Weston.

"It's rather late," the secretary informed Nancy with a superior air. "Mr. Weston doesn't like to make appointments after three o'clock."

"We've driven here from River Heights," Nancy explained patiently. "Please give him my name."

The young woman vanished into an inner office. The girls sat down on a bench to wait. Five minutes passed.

"Looks as if we're out of luck," George grumbled. "The man probably suspects what we came for and means to get out of it if he possibly can."

She lowered her voice, for at that moment the secretary returned.

"Mr. Weston will see you," she told Nancy. "Step into his office, please."

If Nancy and the other girls expected to meet a defiant Baylor Weston they were mistaken. His every movement disclosed that he was as intensely nervous as he had been the day of the accident.

Mr. Weston recognized Nancy, and it was not necessary for her to state her mission. Evidently her visit had been anticipated.

He motioned the girls to be seated, and still without speaking, the manufacturer reached for the bills which Nancy held in her hand. He glanced at them and a look of relief came over his face.

"Well, that's not half bad," he remarked, relaxing. "I was sure it would be much more."

Nancy expected Mr. Weston to mention his insurance company's paying the amount, but instead he opened his desk drawer and took out a checkbook. As he wrote in it, he said:

"I'm decidedly pleased that the total expense is so small. The last time I crashed into a car it cost me real money, to say nothing of the threatened lawsuit."

"The *last* time?" Nancy echoed with a smile.

"I'm very nervous—excitable," the manufacturer reiterated. "Doctor's right—I shouldn't drive a car."

He handed the check to Nancy. "That covers everything?"

"Yes, and thank you. I hope you'll have no more accidents."

"So do I," Baylor Weston returned with a grimace, "but very likely I shall, unless I get a chauffeur. Hm, that's an idea! I'll make a note of it!"

He reached for a pad, and to the amusement of the girls, scribbled down the memorandum.

"By the way," he remarked, "did you hear how much Raybolt lost in the fire?"

"I don't believe the loss has been estimated," Nancy replied. "Mrs. Raybolt visited the ruins today. She was quite overcome."

"The Raybolts always did hate to lose a penny," the manufacturer grunted.

"It wasn't that," Nancy told him. "Mrs. Raybolt declares her husband was in the house at the time of the fire. She believes he was burned to death."

Baylor Weston shook his head doubtfully. "Can't make me believe that Felix Raybolt was caught in that fire. He's too foxy for that! If he has disappeared, you may wager it was for a purpose."

"Mrs. Raybolt's grief seemed to be genuine," Nancy commented.

"No doubt. Raybolt wasn't the fellow to confide in his wife about anything. He kept his own council."

"You knew him well."

"At one time. We broke off business relations years ago. Raybolt was too tricky—mean and unfair in all his dealings. He'd steal ideas without a qualm."

"So I've heard," Nancy returned dryly. "By the way," she asked, "do you have a man by the name of Joe Swenson working for you?"

Mr. Weston thought for a moment, then said, "The name is not familiar to me, but I'll inquire of our personnel office." He called the manager. After a few moments' pause, the answer came back—no.

Nancy was disappointed. She thanked Mr. Weston and the three girls arose. They left the factory and walked to the car.

"Let's take the longer route back to River Heights rather than the Sunview Mountain road," Bess pleaded, and Nancy consented.

As she reached the Weston plant's main gate at the highway, the girls saw that traffic had become heavy.

"Everyone must be coming to town for the carnival," George observed. "I saw the posters advertising it when we drove through Stanford. There's to be some sort of parade, too."

The steady stream of vehicles held the convertible at the entrance of the factory grounds. While the girls were impatiently waiting for a break in the line, the plant whistle blew.

"Now there *will* be a jam!" Nancy exclaimed.

A moment later she finally managed to turn into the highway, but the cars in front of her moved slowly. Again Nancy was forced to halt.

The blowing of the whistle had released hundreds of workmen. They came pouring from the plant. While she waited for the car ahead to move, Nancy watched the men with interest.

Suddenly a vaguely familiar figure caught her eye. At first Nancy thought she must be mistaken, but as the man turned his face toward her, she knew her first impression had been correct.

"Look!" Nancy cried excitedly. "There's the man I saw running away from the fire! He's Joe Swenson!"

CHAPTER XI

Lost in the Crowd

"Joe Swenson!" Bess and George exclaimed simultaneously. "Where?"

"He's crossing the highway!" Nancy pointed. "The man with the blue shirt. Don't take your eyes off him for a second! We must keep him in sight!"

The cars ahead had started to move again and Nancy turned her attention to driving, while Bess and George watched Joe Swenson. They kept close behind him for nearly a block, then George called out that he had turned a corner.

Nancy stopped for a red traffic light, and when she finally turned into the side street, the man was a considerable distance ahead.

"He's walking fast," Bess observed. "We'll lose him if we aren't careful."

The street was crooked and narrow. Children

were playing ball and Nancy was forced to drive with extra caution.

Joe Swenson turned into another street, narrower than the first and rather dingy. Nancy rapidly drew nearer to him, only to lose him again as he cut through an alley.

"Does he know we're following him?" Bess wondered.

"I don't think so," Nancy answered. "We'll catch him at the next street. I can see where the alley ends."

Rubbish, tin cans, and boxes littered the alley, and she did not care to risk a punctured tire. Turning the car, she retraced her route, rounded the block, and reached the opposite end of the alley in time to see Joe Swenson heading toward one of the main streets of Stanford.

"We have him now," Nancy said confidently.

Scarcely had she spoken when the girls noticed that the block directly ahead had been roped off. The sidewalks were lined with pedestrians, and policemen were turning automobiles into side streets.

"What's this?" Nancy asked impatiently.

"It must be the parade," George declared. "And there goes Joe Swenson, heading that way!"

"We'll lose him sure!" Nancy groaned.

True to her prediction, the man melted into the crowd. A policeman motioned for Nancy to turn to the right and she had no choice but to comply. At the first opportunity she parked the car and the girls ran back.

In vain they searched through the throngs of people watching the parade. Joe Swenson had disappeared.

"If that isn't a mean break!" Bess fretted.

"I admit it's hopeless," Nancy said slowly. "The best thing to do is come back tomorrow and try to find him."

The girls returned to the car. As they headed for River Heights, George said, "If Joe Swenson works at the Weston plant, why wasn't his name on the personnel records?"

"Maybe we were mistaken, after all," Bess said.

Nancy did not reply for nearly a minute, then she declared, "Girls, I have a hunch."

"About what?" George asked.

"That Joe Swenson works at the factory, all right."

"But they said nobody by that name was there," Bess objected.

Nancy smiled. "For reasons of his own, he could be using another name."

"Like what?" George spoke up.

"Dahl," Nancy answered.

"His mother's maiden name!" Bess declared. "Oh, Nancy, you're a genius!"

"Better not praise me until I've proved my hunch right," Nancy cautioned.

"Will you phone Mr. Weston and ask him?"

"No, Bess. I want to talk to Joe Swenson without his suspecting anything. If he's using an assumed name, it may be because he's hiding something. Suppose he finds out someone has been inquiring for him? He may run away."

"You're right," George agreed.

Reluctantly the girls rode back to River Heights. "See you tomorrow," Nancy told Bess and George as she stopped at their homes. Upon reaching the Drew house, she found Hannah Gruen awaiting her with a message.

"Ned Nickerson has phoned you five times, Nancy," Hannah said with a smile. "It seems that he wants to invite you to a dinner dance. One of his fraternity brothers is giving it—on the spur of the moment—tonight. Ned would like you to call. I have the number."

Nancy's heart was already pounding with excitement as she dialed. Of course she would accept!

"Great!" said Ned. "I was about to give up hope. Can you be ready in an hour?"

"I'll do my best," Nancy replied.

Singing a gay tune, Nancy quickly disrobed, jumped under a shower, and was dressed in three-quarters of an hour.

"You look lovely, Nancy," Mrs. Gruen complimented her.

"Oh, thank you." Nancy surveyed herself in a long mirror. The pale-green chiffon dress was very becoming, and the gold evening shoes she wore set it off to advantage.

Still humming gaily, Nancy went downstairs holding her white wrap. Ned arrived in a few minutes and they drove off in his car. At first conversation was in a light vein, then Ned asked if Nancy had located the Raybolt arsonist yet.

"No. How about you?"

Ned replied, "All I know is what I read in the papers—first, that Mrs. Raybolt remains in a state bordering on collapse. She's firmly convinced her husband lost his life in the fire."

"The police and fire investigators don't think so," Nancy remarked.

"I do have one interesting piece of news. The police are busy working on a new angle. A clue, which they're withholding from the public, is expected to bring about the arrest of the criminal within a day or two."

"Is it possible that the police suspect Joe Swenson?" Nancy asked herself aloud. "If they arrest him, it will ruin all my plans for trying to help his family!"

"You're being very mysterious," Ned complained good-naturedly. "Why would the police suspect Mr. Swenson? How about letting me in on the secret?"

Nancy laughed. "Maybe you shouldn't beg too hard, Ned. You may find yourself being called upon to do all kinds of outlandish sleuthing jobs."

"I'm at your service," Ned replied quickly.

Little by little, Nancy told him the details. When she had finished, Ned said, "You've certainly done some terrific detective work! Well, good luck tomorrow. Wish I could be with you, but I'm slated to go on an all-day trip with my dad."

Nancy and Ned reached the home of his fraternity brother. Sounds of popular songs being sung in harmony by the guests drifted out. Laughingly, the couple hastened their steps.

All the boys and girls were strangers to Nancy, but she liked them at once. She found them intelligent and full of fun, and they quickly made her feel as if she had always been part of the group.

At the long dinner table the boy on her right, Phil Roberts, proved to be very entertaining. He told several amusing and true stories about strange letters which had come to the attention of the post office.

"Where did you hear about these letters?" Nancy asked him, after the laughter had subsided.

"Oh, my father's the Stanford postmaster," Phil explained. "He told me."

Immediately Nancy wondered if Phil could

have heard anything to shed light on the reason why Mrs. Swenson was not receiving mail from her husband. It took Nancy nearly five minutes to formulate a diplomatic question.

Finally she said, "If someone's mail isn't being delivered, what could be the reason?"

Phil smiled. "Two that I can think of. First, no one is writing to the person, and second, his mail is being stolen." Suddenly he looked intently at Nancy. "What made you ask me that question?"

"Because I know someone who should be getting mail but isn't. If there were money or checks in the letters, a thief might steal them."

"A certain kind of thief would. Say, Nancy, I'm going to tell you something—it's kind of confidential—but I think it might help your friend."

Nancy listened intently for the secret she was about to hear.

CHAPTER XII

Incriminating Evidence

"FOR several weeks," Phil began, "my father and a good many other postmasters have been receiving reports like the one you've just told me, Nancy. The police and the Postal Inspectors Division have been investigating but haven't caught anyone yet."

"Hm," said Nancy. "Then my friend could easily be one of the victims."

Just then a record of dance music began to play and Ned claimed Nancy. For the remainder of the evening there was no chance to resume the conversation about stolen letters. But throughout the evening, the matter was constantly on her mind. By the time the party was over and she had said good night to Ned, the young sleuth had a theory about the thefts. To start solving this mystery, she must first talk to Joe Swenson.

By ten the following morning Nancy was on her way, with Bess and George in the front seat of the car with her. In her purse was the diary. The cousins were intrigued when Nancy told them about the dinner dance.

"Lucky you!" said Bess, pretending to pout. "Couldn't Ned have found a couple of blind dates for George and me?"

Nancy laughed, then turning serious, said, "If we find Joe Swenson, I'm going to ask him point-blank if he has mailed any letters containing money to his wife."

She did not explain her reason for this, not wishing to betray Phil's confidence about the money, money orders, and checks being stolen from mail.

"Suppose he says yes," George suggested.

"Then I'll ask him where he mails his letters and try a little detective work to see what happens."

The first shift of noonday lunchers was trickling from Mr. Weston's factory as Nancy parked nearby. Soon the recreation area was filled with men. Some seated themselves on the ground to eat. Others began to play ball.

"It won't be easy to find Joe Swenson in such a large group," Nancy declared in disappointment. "If we had arrived fifteen minutes earlier, we could have spotted him as he came out of the building."

Nevertheless, the girls eagerly scanned the faces of the workmen. A number of them had gathered near a drinking fountain, but Joe Swenson was not among this group. Not discouraged, the girls began to walk about, inquiring for a man named Dahl. The men they questioned had never heard of him.

"I'm sure he works here," Nancy declared to her friends.

Workmen passing to and fro stared curiously at the girls, obviously wondering what had brought them to the electronics plant.

Nancy was becoming a bit disheartened, when she chanced to observe a light-haired man leaning dejectedly against the high fence which surrounded the grounds. Apparently the man had picked an isolated, tree-shaded spot, away from the other workers. He had his back to the girls, but from a distance Nancy thought his tall, spare build was exactly like that of the stranger she had seen running away from the fire. Could he be Honey's father?

She watched expectantly, and presently the man turned around. He was the same person she had seen on the previous day's visit to the factory. Nancy could not mistake the face—he was Joe Swenson.

"You girls stay here a moment, will you?" Nancy requested. "I think I've found our man. I must speak to him alone. Be on your guard, and if he tries to escape, block the exit to the grounds. I don't think he'll make a disturbance, but if he's guilty, he may attempt a getaway!"

Nancy's heart beat faster than usual as she approached the man who was leaning against the fence. His downcast manner, the girl thought, could mean a guilty conscience.

"I beg your pardon," Nancy said courageously, "but aren't you Mr. Joe Swenson—alias Dahl?"

The man wheeled around, but held his ground. After the first start of surprise, Nancy thought he did not look unusually disturbed at the sudden encounter.

"Yes," he replied, "Dahl's my name. Anything I can do for you?"

For a moment Nancy was at a loss for words. She had half expected that Joe Swenson would be defiant and sullen—not a sad-eyed, kindly man. He looked to her as though he could not have harmed anyone in his life.

"It's all a mistake," Nancy told herself joyfully. "Mr. Swenson is innocent. He didn't start the Raybolt fire."

The next moment she had regained her composure and was again the impartial, businesslike detective. She showed him her driver's license for identification.

"I have news of your wife," Nancy said to him quietly.

"Helen?" the man demanded eagerly, his face lighting up. "She's not ill, I hope!"

"Oh, no," Nancy assured him, "but she's dreadfully worried about you and is trying to locate you."

"I don't understand," Joe Swenson said, frowning. "I sent my address but didn't want to go home until—er—a certain matter was cleared up."

"Then you *have* written to your wife?" Nancy questioned.

"Yes, twice. I sent her two good-sized money orders."

For a second Nancy wondered if he was telling the truth. Looking him straight in the eye, she said, "Mrs. Swenson never received them."

"What!" her husband exclaimed in such genuine astonishment that Nancy had no further doubts.

"They need money badly," Nancy said, and summoned her friends to come forward. She introduced Bess and George, then repeated what Joe Swenson had told her.

"Your letters have been *stolen!*" George said vehemently.

"But how? Where?" the inventor cried out. "I mailed them in the post office myself!"

No one could answer this puzzle. Suddenly he pulled an unsealed envelope from his pocket.

"Here is another letter to my wife with twenty-five dollars in it. I was going to send a money order today. Would you be so kind as to deliver this in person?"

"I'll be glad to," Nancy answered, smiling, and tucked the envelope in her pocket.

She then changed the subject to obtain more information on another topic. "Would you mind telling us, Mr. Swenson, why you're using the name Dahl here?"

"Certainly. I'm an inventor, and I've had hard luck. The name Joe Swenson seems to have brought trouble. My mother's people were always successful. On the spur of the moment I decided to use that name here. A man I know vouched for me, since I didn't have any references to give."

"I see," said Nancy. She smiled disarmingly. "Your wife told me of some unfair dealings you've had with a man who buys patents."

"Indeed they were unfair. He cheated me. Felix Raybolt is a thief!"

The three girls were unprepared for such an outburst from this seemingly mild-mannered man. Apparently he guessed what was going through their minds.

"I shouldn't burden you with my problems," he said apologetically. "Things aren't any easier, even though I have a job. Did you know the Raybolt house burned?"

"Yes."

"To be truthful I am afraid I may be blamed if anyone finds out I was there."

"You were there?" Bess asked, a look of feigned innocence in her big blue eyes.

"I had an appointment with Mr. Raybolt early that evening," Joe Swenson explained. "The house was dark. I had just rung the bell when there was a terrific explosion inside the house, and it burst into flames. I called and called to Mr. Raybolt—but there was no answer."

"Did you try to break in to help?" George asked bluntly.

"Yes, but I couldn't budge the front door. I ran around to the back. Because of the flames, I knew I couldn't do any good. Then I heard a car approaching the house. It occurred to me I might be blamed, so I ran away."

"Did you see anyone on the grounds?" Nancy asked.

"No."

"Do you think Mr. Raybolt lost his life in the fire?" Nancy asked.

"I really don't know. I didn't see or hear him inside, and the police haven't located any evidence," the inventor replied.

Nancy had been endeavoring to formulate an honest opinion of the man's story. Her hand went to her purse but she did not bring forth the diary. From their casual conversation so far, she could not be absolutely certain that Joe Swenson was innocent. She must question him further.

"They've been searching the grounds for clues," Nancy said nonchalantly. "A number of articles have been picked up in the vicinity."

Swenson looked sharply at Nancy, as though it had dawned on him that he indeed might be under suspicion. However, his next words were spoken casually.

"I wonder if a diary was found. I lost one. Probably dropped it along the road."

Nancy made no move to give him the diary, although she was convinced that it was his.

"I hated to lose that little journal," Joe Swenson continued. "It was written mostly in Swedish and wouldn't be of any value except to myself— and to Felix Raybolt. That sly fox!"

"What has the diary to do with Mr. Raybolt?" Nancy asked.

"The diary contains—" Joe Swenson hesitated. "Well, it contains things Felix Raybolt wishes were not written down. That man cheated me out of a fortune, but I haven't a chance to prove my case without the diary and without money to retain a lawyer. To make matters worse, I've even lost a ring I treasured highly."

He made a hopeless gesture and lapsed into gloomy silence.

Again Nancy's hand went to the diary in her purse. Again she hesitated. Suppose Joe Swenson *were* guilty, and she was withholding evidence from the police! Nancy made a quick decision: to hold onto the journal until the truth was learned.

Before she could question the man further, the return-to-work whistle blew a shrill blast.

"I must go now," Swenson said hurriedly.

"When are you off duty?" Nancy asked.

"Four o'clock."

"Then perhaps we'll see you again before we return to River Heights." Noticing the man's surprise, she added quickly, "Wouldn't you like me to carry a message to Mrs. Swenson and Honey?"

"Thank you. But I'll write to them again."

Nancy and her friends watched him until he had disappeared inside the building. The girls then walked slowly back to the car.

"I'll bet," said George, "that Joe Swenson is worried about the fire, and will run away again."

Nancy remained silent, in deep thought. Just as she reached the convertible someone grabbed her arm roughly. She turned to face a tough, cruel-looking man.

CHAPTER XIII

The Law Takes Over

"LET go of me!" Nancy cried out, and tried to shake off the man's iron grip. When she did not succeed, Bess and George started pounding the man and forced him to release Nancy's arm.

"What do you want?" Nancy demanded indignantly.

"Some information. Why are you snooping around here?" the stranger snarled.

"Are you a factory guard?" Nancy countered, knowing from his clothes and manner that he most certainly was not.

"Why—uh—yes. That's what I am. And I got a right to know why you been talkin' to that workman."

"The conversation was private," Nancy told the man firmly. "Now if you'll just move—"

For a moment the obnoxious stranger did not

seem inclined to do so, but finally he strode off down the street. The girls stepped into the car and drove away.

"Nancy, aren't you worried?" Bess asked. "That man was positively horrible."

"Yes, I am, Bess. Because I'm more certain than ever that Joe Swenson is in some kind of jam."

"If we can see him at four o'clock, I'm going to ask him about that crude person," declared George. "Say, Nancy, where are you going now?"

"Yes, where?" Bess echoed. "I'm starving!"

Nancy laughed. "I could use some lunch myself. After that, I'll introduce myself to Phil Roberts' father."

"The Stanford postmaster!" Bess exclaimed. "Nancy, you're not transferring your affections from Ned to Phil already!"

"Nothing like that," Nancy assured her with a grin. "I have a little scheme I'd like to try out and I need his cooperation."

Nancy stopped speaking as she drove into a public parking lot next to a tearoom. The girls went inside and were fortunate to be seated at the last available table. It was such a noisy place that the girls did not try to talk.

Half an hour later they came out of the tearoom, glad to breathe the fresh air and escape the din. Since the post office was close by, the girls walked there. Seeing a door sign marked:

PRIVATE
POSTMASTER

Nancy went to it and knocked. Presently it was opened by a pleasant, middle-aged man.

"I'm Nancy Drew from River Heights," she said, smiling. "I met your son Phil at a party."

"Oh, yes! Phil told me. Won't you come in?"

After the girls had entered and the door had been closed, Nancy introduced her friends.

"I've come on an unusual errand, Mr. Roberts," Nancy said. "A man I know who works at Stanford Electronics has sent two letters containing money orders from here. Neither has been received. Probably all your employees are above suspicion, but would you mind if I make a little experiment?"

The postmaster smiled. "What kind of experiment?"

"I'll mail a note to the man's wife with a money order in it from your office," Nancy explained. "Could you possibly find out if that letter *is* sent out from here?"

Mr. Roberts looked intently at Nancy. "You're a very ingenious young lady," he remarked. "And if the letter *does* leave here, then you'll check with the receiving post office to find out if it has reached there?"

"Yes. The family of this man is desperately in need of receiving money from him. I'm trying to help them."

"And I'll help too," the postmaster said suddenly. "Now, will you please give me the name and address of this woman?"

Nancy took Joe Swenson's unsealed envelope from her purse and Mr. Roberts copied the two names and addresses on it. As he handed it back, he said, "Mail this at once." Then he added, "If you come back in a couple of hours, I'll have a report for you—after I personally examine all the outgoing mailbags."

"I'll be here." Nancy thanked the postmaster and the three girls went into the main lobby. There, Nancy bought the twenty-five-dollar money order, kept the purchaser's receipt, and tucked the other section, properly filled out, into the letter. Then she sealed the envelope and slipped the letter into the nearby slot.

When the girls reached the street, Bess said, "That was a daring thing to do, Nancy. Suppose the letter is intercepted, and the money order cashed by some unscrupulous person?"

"If that happens, I'll make good on the money. Right now, tell me, where are we going to spend two hours?"

George suggested attending a movie across the street, and the girls went into the theater. They became so interested in the historical mystery film that the time flew by. The feature ended just as the two hours were up, and the girls hurried back to Mr. Roberts' office.

Again he opened the door. The postmaster was not alone. A policeman stood guarding a man who sat dejectedly in a chair, his face in his hands. He looked up at Nancy, hate blazing in his eyes. *The money-order clerk!*

"Nancy Drew, thank you for leading us to this thief!" the postmaster said. "Ralph Ringman has confessed to taking not only the letter you mailed, but all money orders of any size. He has two accomplices, a man and a woman, who go to various towns and cash the money orders."

"I'm not the only employee in on this deal," Ringman cried out.

Mr. Roberts smiled. "I figured that might be the case, and have notified other postmasters who have had complaints of undelivered money orders to try the same ruse that Nancy Drew suggested."

At that moment the phone rang. Mr. Roberts answered it. "Yes, Clyde. . . . You did? . . . Good! I guess that little racket is over with."

When he hung up, Mr. Roberts reported to the others that Ringman's outside accomplices had just been arrested by the police and had confessed their parts in the scheme.

On a hunch, Nancy told about the rough-looking man who had questioned her. "Was he in league with Ralph Ringman?" she asked the postmaster.

"That's right." Mr. Roberts turned to the

"Nancy Drew, thank you for leading us to this thief," said the postmaster

prisoner. "You'll be interested to hear that your pal meant to double-cross you. He planned to hold up Swenson at the plant and grab Swenson's money for himself. Just as he was about to emerge from his hiding place in the shrubbery nearby, Miss Drew and her friends came along. When he overheard the conversation about the stolen mail, he got panicky. That's why he followed Miss Drew and accused her of snooping."

"The low-down sneak!" snarled Ringman.

Mr. Roberts said that a man from the Postal Inspectors Division would take custody of the prisoner. "By the way," he said to Nancy, "do you still want Mr. Swenson's letter sent?"

"Yes, if it's safe. I'll give the money order receipt to him." Nancy glanced at her watch. "We must hurry," she said. "Thank you, Mr. Roberts. Please give my regards to Phil."

The girls hurried off. At a traffic light they paused, waiting for it to turn green. Behind them stood two men conversing in low voices.

"Where'd you get the tip?" one asked.

"From Raybolt's wife. She said the man who set fire to the house had an appointment with him there that evening."

"I heard he ran away. Where'd he go?"

"Nobody knows. But we tracked him here. He's working at the electronics factory under an assumed name."

"What is it?"

"We don't know. But we have the man's description. We'll have him in jail by tonight!"

Nancy, Bess, and George hardly breathed during this recital. Did these men mean Joe Swenson?

CHAPTER XIV

An Arrest

THE traffic light turned green and the three girls began to cross the street. Nancy made a point of staying in front of the two men who had said they were going to see that someone, presumably Joe Swenson, was arrested.

"Who are these men?" she wondered. "Detectives? Or are they in the employ of Raybolt? If Mr. Swenson is innocent, he mustn't be sent to jail!"

Nancy immediately made up her mind what she would do: meet Honey's father if possible, show him the diary, and ask him to translate some of it. "Then I'll decide what to do next, and whether or not to warn Mr. Swenson of his possibly being arrested. He and his family shouldn't have to suffer such disgrace if it's unwarranted!"

When the girls reached the opposite curb,

Nancy took her friends' arms and whispered, "Come on! Hurry! We have work to do!"

They ran to Nancy's car. Nancy handed the keys to George. "Will you drive, so I'll be free to hop out and get hold of Mr. Swenson the instant he comes to the gate?"

George took the wheel and they made record time to the factory. She parked in the first space beyond the front of the gate, and left the engine running.

"You girls watch for those men we overheard. I'll look for Joe Swenson," Nancy directed.

As she spoke, the four-o'clock whistle blew.

"He'll be out any minute now!" George exclaimed.

Anxiously the girls scanned the faces of the workmen as they came from the building. "Where *is* he?" Bess fretted.

At that moment Nancy caught sight of the inventor. She alighted and called his name. With a smile of friendly recognition, he came over to the car.

"Jump in!" Nancy invited, indicating the rear seat. "We'll give you a lift."

"Why, thanks," the inventor returned gratefully. "I live on the south side. Another fellow and I share a room at the outskirts of town. I imagine it's out of your way—"

"Not at all," Nancy assured him with a worried glance up and down the street.

In her haste to leave the plant area, Nancy climbed in and almost pulled the man in after her. She asked George to press the button to roll up the convertible's top.

"A man certainly appreciates a ride home after a hard day on his feet," Swenson remarked, leaning back against the cushion. "I'm not yet accustomed to standing eight hours, but I'll be all right in a week or so. I'm glad to earn a little money by any means, after being out of work for so long."

As George drove down the street, Nancy said, "Mr. Swenson, the mystery about your lost letters has been solved." Quickly she explained about the mail clerk who had been arrested.

The inventor was shocked, and shook his head sadly. "I'm glad he has been caught. But what an unfortunate thing for him to do. He probably has a family—they'll have to suffer with him. Crimes, big or little, are so useless. Whatever profits they may bring are always temporary."

Nancy nodded. She was becoming more convinced every minute that Joe Swenson was an honest person!

"I have another surprise," she said. "Your diary was picked up near the drive to the Raybolt house." She took the journal from her handbag. "Would you mind translating some of the Swedish for me?"

"My diary! Oh, how lucky!" Almost affectionately he began to turn the pages. "Here is an item about Honey's birthday. How she loved the little toy I made for her! I was always planning to try to market those mechanical dolls, but I never got to it."

George interrupted to ask which direction to take, and Nancy said, "Oh, let's just ride out into the country."

She wanted to elude the men who intended to arrest Mr. Swenson until she could make up her mind what to do. Suddenly the inventor's face darkened. "Here's a note about Felix Raybolt." He translated, " 'I have been warned by my friend Anson Heilberg not to let Raybolt see my invention but I shall take a chance. I must because I need money for rent and food. He will give me an advance.' "

Mr. Swenson remarked bitterly, "How I wish I had listened to Anson! Felix Raybolt would not give me another cent or any part of a royalty from the use of my electrochemical process for putting a ceramic finish on steel!"

"How terribly unfair!" Bess cried out, and the other girls expressed the same opinion.

Nancy then told the inventor that a friend of hers had found the signet ring. "I'll see that it is returned to you," Nancy assured him.

"Well, that *is* good news," said Mr. Swenson.

Nancy gradually switched the conversation to the Raybolt fire, and said, "The investigators report that the explosions in the house could have been caused by a freak accident: a television set not working properly; a defective electronic heating device setting off some kind of explosive stored in the cellar. Mr. Swenson, have you any idea *what* really happened at the Raybolts'?"

Mr. Swenson looked at Nancy searchingly. "My answer might explain a good many angles to the case," he said slowly. "As you probably know, it's against the law to store explosives without a permit. I believe Felix Raybolt was breaking that law. He probably was in the house waiting for me and accidentally caused the explosion himself!"

"But they found no evidence of—of a body," Bess spoke up with a shudder.

"Mr. Raybolt undoubtedly escaped, and then disappeared, knowing he would be arrested," the inventor said vehemently.

"But you didn't *see* him run out?" Nancy queried.

"No."

"We should have looked for footprints, but I guess it's too late now," Nancy remarked.

"Oh, why didn't we think of that!" Bess murmured. She had turned around to watch out the rear window for any pursuers. Suddenly she gasped. "Police!"

George had just passed a side road. From it shot a car with two state troopers. When it turned in their direction, George said grimly, "I hope they're not after us."

All the occupants of the convertible grew tense, but Nancy said, "Just keep going at this same speed. Let's not act guilty."

By this time she was convinced of Mr. Swenson's innocence, and hoped fervently that the officers were not pursuing her car. Nancy doubted they would take her word about the truth of the inventor's story.

"Maybe they're after someone else—for speeding," Bess said, though without conviction.

Nancy stole a glance out the rear window. Her spirits sank. The State Police car was gaining on them, but did not look as though it was going to pass the convertible.

An uneasy thought crossed Nancy's mind. "If those troopers *are* after Joe Swenson, then George, Bess, and I might be arrested for aiding a suspected criminal to escape!"

George was forced to slow down for a sharp curve. Directly beyond it, two men were driving a small herd of cattle across the highway.

"What luck!" George cried, slowing down.

She honked her horn and tried to edge through, but only succeeded in frightening the cows so that they stood motionless. The convertible came to a halt. Behind it, the police car drew nearer.

Nancy had a sudden impulse to tell Joe Swenson to duck down out of sight, then checked herself. Such an action would indeed make the officers suspicious. Instead, she slipped the diary into her handbag.

Nancy glanced at her companion. Mr. Swenson's face was grim. The police car pulled up alongside the convertible. Nancy's heart was in her throat, but she tried not to show any agitation.

The two herdsmen had headed the cows off to the side of the road. Affecting nonchalance, George started to drive off. But a shout from the troopers' car stopped her.

"Hold on!" one of the officers cried out. "Pull over!"

"They *were* following us," Bess groaned.

Quickly Nancy whispered to Joe Swenson, "Don't worry. We'll stick by you."

The officers had jumped out. They strode up to the convertible.

"We've had a call to pick up this car," said one, while the other thrust his face through the open rear-door window and peered intently at Mr. Swenson.

"This is the man!" he declared.

"What do you mean?" Nancy demanded coolly, with as much conviction as she could muster.

"Are you Joe Swenson?" the trooper barked, ignoring Nancy's question.

"Yes."

"You are wanted by the Mapleton police for deliberately setting the Raybolt house on fire."

At this accusation the girls gasped and Joe Swenson blanched. Then a flush of anger mounted to his cheeks.

"What nonsense is this? You haven't a shred of proof. I don't know anything about the fire. You have the wrong man."

"Well, you can explain that at headquarters. You'll have to come along with us. The less trouble you make, the better it will go for you."

One of the troopers flipped a pair of handcuffs from his pocket. Joe Swenson shrank back.

"Don't put them on, please! I'll come without any trouble."

"O.K. But don't try any funny stunts. Climb out and be quick about it!"

"Just a minute, Officer," Nancy interposed. "Aren't you making a mistake? I feel sure Mr. Swenson isn't the man you're after. Please let him go free. I'll be responsible for his appearance in court."

Joe Swenson added, "I started working at Baylor Weston's factory just recently. I don't mind answering your questions, but if I'm detained in jail, I'll lose my job."

Protest was useless. Joe Swenson gave Nancy a courageous, apologetic smile, and alighted.

"You girls will have to come along too!" the officer announced. "Drive on ahead, and not too fast! You have some explaining to do too. Don't try to get away!"

CHAPTER XV

Nancy Is Accused

"This is an outrage!" Bess gasped. "You mean we actually must go to police headquarters?"

"I'm sorry I involved you girls in this," Joe Swenson murmured. He turned pleadingly to the officers. "It wasn't their fault. They merely offered me a ride."

"They'll all have to come to headquarters for questioning," the officer insisted.

Mr. Swenson was escorted to the State Police car. Before the troopers started off, they again cautioned George to drive ahead slowly.

"For two cents I *would* step on the gas and try to get away!" she fumed to her companions.

"I wouldn't advise it," Bess said uneasily. "We're in enough trouble now."

"Oh, Bess! I was only kidding," George retorted.

The three girls fell into gloomy silence. The prospect of unpleasant notoriety for their families was anything but reassuring. The friends were glad that at least they had been permitted to drive a short way ahead of the police car, for their entry into Mapleton attracted less attention than would otherwise have been the case.

When they reached headquarters and parked, Nancy warned, "Whatever happens, don't say anything that will incriminate Joe Swenson!"

Outside the building, the girls were confronted by the two men they had overheard talking in Stanford.

"This is our man, all right!" one of them said as the troopers' car bearing Joe Swenson pulled up. The inventor was hustled out, and into the custody of the men.

"Trying to help Swenson make a getaway, eh?" the other of the pair accused the girls. "Come along, you three!"

"Plain-clothes detectives!" Nancy murmured.

As they went up the steps, George teased, "What would Ned Nickerson think if he could see his Nancy now!"

"If it comes to the worst, we can call on him." Nancy smiled. "Before we're through, you may be glad he is my friend!"

Inside headquarters, the situation lost all suggestion of humor. Here Nancy and her friends were told by Police Captain Johnson that the detectives had learned at the plant of Joe Swenson's departure in a car bearing Nancy's license number. He made no reference to the detectives' source of information. To the girls' dismay, the inventor was booked on a charge of arson.

No charge was placed against them, but the girls were asked a great many questions, and their names and addresses were written down. When Nancy gave hers, significant looks were exchanged among the captain and the detectives, Davil and Rock. After that, the girls were treated less peremptorily.

But if they had hoped that the name of Drew would release them at once, Nancy and the cousins were disappointed. They were informed that they must submit to further questioning.

George and Bess were thoroughly frightened and Joe Swenson had become so agitated that he could not speak in a normal tone of voice. Nancy realized that he was in no condition to defend himself. The four were given chairs opposite the two stern-faced detectives and their captain.

One could have heard a pin drop, the room became so quiet. The officers stared fixedly at Joe Swenson, who squirmed uncomfortably in his chair. Suddenly Detective Davil pointed an accusing finger, and his voice rasped out so sharply that Nancy jumped.

"Swenson, when did you first plot the death of Felix Raybolt?"

"When did I— I don't know what you mean," Mr. Swenson stammered.

The keen glance of his questioner did not waver.

"You know well enough what I mean. It won't do you any good to try to lie. You were seen near the Raybolt estate on the day of the fire."

"Who says I was there?" Swenson demanded. "You're accusing me because you can't find the real criminal!"

His shot went home, for the detective blinked, briefly nonplused. But he went on, "You were seen by the railroad station agent, and as soon as he identifies you, we'll have you behind bars. Now out with your story! It will go easier for you if you make a complete confession."

"There's nothing to confess," Swenson returned bitterly. "I *did* go to the Raybolt estate—"

Nancy's heart began to pound. Was the inventor going to confess something he had not told her?

"So!" his questioner cried triumphantly. "Then you admit going to the house!"

"I've admitted nothing damaging!" Swenson retorted hotly. "I went to the house because I had an appointment with Felix Raybolt."

Nancy was sure now that Swenson intended to make a clean breast of everything; and while admiring his honesty, she realized that he was apt to make his case appear worse than it might be. She longed to warn him to remain silent until he could consult a lawyer.

Bess and George sat transfixed.

"So you had an appointment with Raybolt, eh?" Detective Rock took up the questioning. "What kind of appointment?"

"He had a patent of mine and I wanted him to make a settlement."

"Raybolt owed you money?"

"Yes. He stole my invention. I wanted either the money, or my drawings back."

"What did Raybolt say?"

"I never saw him. There were no lights in the house. He didn't answer the bell. Then there was an explosion and I ran away."

"You knew he was in the house and you didn't try to save him?" the captain interjected.

"I don't believe he *was* in the house!"

"When did you last see Raybolt?"

"In a restaurant here in town."

"I see," Detective Davil observed with satisfaction. "You had an argument, didn't you?"

"Yes," Swenson admitted unwillingly, "we *did* have hot words."

"Which ended in a threat from you," the officer concluded.

Joe Swenson shook his head vehemently. "No, I swear it! I'll tell you everything—right from the very beginning. Raybolt seemed uneasy, as though he were afraid I'd attempt physical violence—he had a guilty conscience, all right!"

"You argued about the invention?"

"Yes. He admitted he had deliberately stolen my ideas, but he defied me to prove anything. That made me angry."

"You threatened him?"

"I told him I would take the matter to court. Of course I didn't have any money to engage a lawyer, but my bluff frightened Raybolt and he told me to come to the house where we could talk privately."

"What do you think caused the fire?" the captain asked.

"The explosion—which nearly knocked me off my feet. I was sort of dazed for several minutes—"

"What happened next?"

"It came over me that if I were found near the place I might be accused of causing the fire. When I heard a car coming up the driveway, I decided to make a getaway. I scrambled through the hedge and ran into the woods."

"You're sure you didn't leave Raybolt inside on purpose?" Detective Rock asked.

"A thousand times, no!" Mr. Swenson cried out indignantly. "I hated that man, I'll admit, but I didn't plot his death."

"Why didn't you tell your story right away?"

"I was afraid it would be misinterpreted. I had no idea Raybolt was missing until I read it in the newspaper."

The three officials took turns questioning Swenson. They quizzed him about details and time but were unable to confuse him.

Nancy was certain that the inventor's account was true, yet she had to acknowledge that the story sounded somewhat implausible. The fact remained that Felix Raybolt was missing and that Joe Swenson was the last person known to have an appointment with him.

Nevertheless, the inventor's straightforward manner had impressed the officers, and Nancy thought they were on the verge of letting him go. Felix Raybolt had been generally disliked, and it was common knowledge that he *had* made his fortune by ruthlessly adopting the ideas of various inventors.

The three officials held a whispered conference, then began questioning Nancy and her friends. The girls told no more than was necessary, with Nancy stressing the story of the inventor's lost letters and the thieving mail clerk. She put in a good word for Mr. Swenson at every opportunity, and it was apparent that she was creating a favorable impression.

The unpleasant session was drawing to a close, with every prospect of vindication for Joe Swenson, when there was a knock at the door.

An officer entered, addressing himself to his superior. "Mrs. Raybolt is here now. Shall I send her in?"

As an affirmative answer was given, Nancy exchanged despairing glances with her friends. She sensed that since Mrs. Raybolt had set the detectives on Joe Swenson's trail, the woman would create a scene. "I'm sure she'll do all in her power to damage his case," Nancy thought.

Her premonition was correct. Mrs. Raybolt's very appearance aroused the sympathy of the officials. The woman evidently had worried herself into a state bordering on nervous collapse and the sight of Joe Swenson made her distraught.

"Can you identify him?" the police captain asked.

Mrs. Raybolt stopped sobbing long enough to take her first good look at the prisoner. Nancy, who was watching her closely, saw uncertainty flash over her face. The young detective was convinced the woman had never seen Mr. Swenson before in her life!

Mrs. Raybolt hesitated only an instant, then cried hysterically, "Yes, I'm sure this is the man my husband went to meet—Felix feared him. He is a heartless criminal who deliberately burned my home and plotted my husband's death!"

She burst into tears again and an officer led her from the room. However, the damage had been done. If the three officials had ever seriously considered freeing Swenson, the decision was instantly changed.

"You girls are free to go," the captain told

Nancy and her friends. "If we need you again, we'll summon you."

"What about Mr. Swenson?" Nancy inquired hopefully.

"We'll have to lock him up. Sorry if he's a friend of yours. His story may be on the level, but he'll have to prove it."

There was nothing more to be said. Joe Swenson thanked Nancy for her interest in his case.

"You're the only real friend I have," he said unhappily. "I've told them the truth, but they won't believe me."

"If you only had a witness!" Nancy murmured. "Someone who saw you at the door."

"No one was around," Mr. Swenson returned gloomily. "The place was deserted."

"Don't give up hope," Nancy said encouragingly. "I'll find a lawyer for you. And I'll bring your wife and Honey to see you, too."

The conversation was abruptly cut short as an officer took the prisoner by the arm and led him away.

When they entered the outside room, Nancy and her friends found Mrs. Raybolt, slumped on a bench, sobbing. Nancy, provoked that the woman had testified unfairly against Joe Swenson, started to pass her without a word. Then pity surmounted indignation and she paused.

"Don't grieve about your husband," Nancy

pleaded. "He'll be found alive—I feel confident of it."

Mrs. Raybolt wiped her eyes and stood up. She glared at Nancy with an almost insane look in her eyes.

"You dare to tell me that!" she cried out. "You're an accomplice of Joe Swenson! My husband is gone! You probably helped plot his death!"

Mrs. Raybolt slapped Nancy's face, then began to shake the girl by her shoulders.

"Captain," she screamed, "come here! I demand that you arrest this—this accomplice!"

CHAPTER XVI

A New Assignment

SHOCKED by Mrs. Raybolt's angry outburst, Nancy stepped back to dodge the blows.

Bess and George had jumped forward to her defense. But just then a sergeant burst into the room and interceded. Mrs. Raybolt stopped fighting with her fists but not with her tongue.

"I demand the arrest of this girl! She's in league with Joe Swenson and helped to kill my husband!" she screamed.

At this point Captain Johnson appeared. "Mrs. Raybolt," he said sternly, "the law will handle this case. I advise you to calm down or you may find yourself in a hospital under the care of a psychiatrist."

The distraught woman started to reply to this, but apparently thought better of it.

Nancy said calmly, "Mrs. Raybolt, I don't blame you for being upset. But please try to believe that people are trying to help find your husband. The fire investigators are sure no one was in your home at the time of the explosion and fire. Therefore, Mr. Raybolt must be alive."

"Then where is he?" Mrs. Raybolt demanded.

"No one knows." Nancy looked directly at the woman. "Unless *you* do," she added disarmingly.

Mrs. Raybolt gave a startled quiver. Then she sank into a chair and covered her face with her hands. The others in the room looked at one another. Was the answer going to be yes or no?

Nancy had a strong hunch that it should be yes, but that as soon as Mrs. Raybolt recovered from the shock of Nancy's unexpected question, she would say no. Finally the woman raised her head. She did not have the look of a grief-stricken widow. Instead, she glared balefully at Nancy.

"This girl is crazy," she said. "Another one of those meddling teen-agers. Why doesn't she stay out of other people's business? Of course I haven't heard from Felix. How could I? He's dead! I tell you he's dead!" Mrs. Raybolt's voice had risen to a high pitch.

Captain Johnson asked a sergeant to take Mrs. Raybolt to her car, but requested that the girls remain. After the woman had gone, the officer asked Nancy what had prompted her question.

The girl detective smiled. "I'm sure that many other people think Mr. Raybolt is alive. He has the reputation of having cheated people, including poor Mr. Swenson. Talk is going around that he felt it best to disappear. But wouldn't he get in touch with his wife?"

The police captain looked at Nancy in astonishment. "You are a very clear thinker," he said. "The theory that Mr. Raybolt is alive is being worked on. Hospitals, airlines, railroad companies, steamship companies—all have been questioned. No clues have come up yet."

Nancy thanked the officer for the information, then said, "I hope Mr. Raybolt will be found, and when he is, that he will clear Mr. Swenson of any blame in connection with the fire."

The officer did not reply. Nancy turned to Bess and George. "I think we'd better leave now."

When they reached the sidewalk, George said, "Wow! What a session! Where do we go from here?"

"Home," Bess replied. "What a day this has been!"

"Do you insist?" Nancy asked.

Bess eyed her chum intently. "What's on your mind?"

"I was wondering if Mr. Weston could help us clear Joe Swenson," Nancy replied. "Do you mind driving back to Stanford with me so I can talk to him?"

"Let's do it," Bess urged. "Anything to help dear little Honey's father."

"I agree," said George.

Nancy slid into the driver's seat and took the

main street which led toward the highway to Stanford. As the car passed one Mapleton store after another, Bess kept gazing at the window displays. Finally she asked Nancy to stop.

"I want to run in and buy a new dress for Honey," she said.

"I'll come with you and get her some underwear," George spoke up.

Nancy chuckled. "I'll follow and pick up some shoes for her. First I'll phone Mr. Weston. If he can see us, I'll call home and tell Hannah to notify your families."

The friends alighted and Nancy hastened into a drug store to make the telephone calls. Then she went to a children's shoe store. When she rejoined the cousins back at the car, the girls showed one another their purchases.

"They're lovely," said Nancy. "These things should make Honey very happy. Glad you thought of it, Bess. Mr. Weston will see us, so let's go!"

They reached the impressive Weston home about six-thirty. Both the manufacturer and his wife were amazed to hear of the arrest of Joe Swenson, known as Joe Dahl.

"Even in the short time Dahl has been working for us, he has become a very valuable man in our organization," the plant owner said. "On my desk is a recommendation from the manager for a promotion."

"Then if he's cleared of this charge against him," said Nancy, "you'll take him back?"

"Yes, indeed."

The young sleuth gave Mr. Weston a warm smile in appreciation, then said, "I wonder if you or your factory manager can give us any information that might help to exonerate Mr. Swenson?"

The manufacturer thought for several seconds, then shook his head. He arose, went to the telephone, and called his plant manager. There was a lengthy conversation, then Mr. Weston came back to report:

"I'm afraid we haven't any clues to help you, but my manager feels certain Mr. Dahl—that is, Swenson—would never resort to seeking revenge on an enemy. He is a highly ethical person. I'd be glad to defend him in this way."

"I'll pass the word along," Nancy said. "Thank you so much." She arose to leave.

At once Mrs. Weston insisted that the girls remain to dinner, an invitation which her husband heartily seconded.

"We wouldn't think of your driving back to River Heights without first having something to eat," he declared.

The girls were persuaded to stay. A four-course dinner was perfectly served by a butler. Mr. and Mrs. Weston were charmingly informal and conversation took on a less serious tone.

Soon after dinner the girls said good-by to the

manufacturer and his wife and headed for River Heights. After taking her friends to their homes, Nancy continued to her own residence. She was surprised to see a familiar car standing at the curb.

"Ned must be here!" she thought. "I wonder if he has any news for me?"

She met the young man on the porch as he was leaving the house.

"Nancy, what luck!" he exclaimed with evident pleasure. "I was afraid you weren't coming."

"Any news?" Nancy inquired hopefully.

Ned shook his head regretfully. "I guess I'm not very good as a detective. I haven't been able to learn anything of value. I just drove over thinking you might like to go to a movie with me."

"I've already seen one today," Nancy said. "And I've had all sorts of adventures. So, if you don't mind, I'd rather stay here and talk. I have a lot to tell you."

The suggestion was not displeasing to Ned, for he had mentioned the show merely as an excuse to spend the evening with Nancy.

"You look tired," he said sympathetically. "I shouldn't have come tonight."

"I'm glad you did," Nancy told him quickly. "There's something I particularly want you to do for me."

"At your service!"

Nancy then recounted to the astounded young

man all that had happened at Stanford and Mapleton.

"Since you live in Mapleton, it will be easy for you to see Joe Swenson," she concluded. "I wish you'd go to the jail and talk with him—try to cheer him up."

"You bet your life I'll go," Ned assured her promptly. "Anything more I can do?"

"Well, tomorrow you might drive over to Sandy Creek and take some packages to Honey." She indicated the gifts now lying on the hall table. "I'd go myself, only I want to concentrate on finding Mr. Raybolt."

"I'll be glad to go. I sure feel sorry for those folks. Tell you what! Suppose I take both of them—Mrs. Swenson and Honey—to see Joe. That should cheer him up a little."

Ned and Nancy discussed the mystery of Felix Raybolt's strange disappearance, and Ned was of the opinion, too, that Raybolt's wife might know more than she was telling. It was his conviction that Raybolt had gone into hiding for some nefarious reason.

Seeing that Nancy was very weary, Ned cut his visit shorter than he had intended. When he left her it was with the promise that he would do all in his power to help her locate Felix Raybolt.

Nancy did not retire immediately. She noticed that a light was burning in her father's study, and she decided to tell him her suspicions. He was buried deep in a lawbook, but he looked up and smiled as his daughter perched herself on the arm of his chair.

"Nancy, you look worried," he observed. "I hope this new case of yours isn't getting you down."

"I'm worried about Joe Swenson," she explained. "What do you think of his chances, Dad?"

"If the account on tonight's newcast is correct, I'm of the opinion he'll be convicted—unless Felix Raybolt shows up."

"That's what I want to talk to you about. I'm sure Mr. Raybolt must be hiding somewhere."

"And I agree," her father said. "Nancy, I obtained one bit of information today that might prove this. I thought you might track it down for me."

CHAPTER XVII

An Important Clue

NANCY could hardly wait for her father to proceed. She left the arm of his chair and seated herself on a couch opposite him.

"As you recall," the lawyer began, "I mentioned that Felix Raybolt practically had stolen my client's invention—an improvement for an automatic elevator."

Nancy leaned forward, listening intently as her father continued, "Mr. Simpson also feels that Raybolt may have decided matters were getting too hot for him and he'd better disappear. The other day Mr. Simpson's wife happened to stop at a country store and gas station a few miles outside of Mapleton.

"A run-down old car with a shabby-looking driver was just pulling away. Mrs. Simpson had only a fleeting glimpse of the man, but she thinks he may have been Mr. Raybolt."

"How exciting!" Nancy exclaimed. "Did she follow him?"

"No, but she asked the attendant about him. The man bought a large quantity of canned goods —including bread in tins."

"Which makes it appear," said Nancy, "that the man was going camping."

"Exactly. Of course he may not have been Mr. Raybolt. The clerks in the store said the shabby-looking customer was a stranger to them. But I think the clue is worth investigating."

"Oh, I agree. The man might have been Mr. Raybolt in disguise!" said Nancy eagerly. "I'll get right to it and start by going to that store first thing tomorrow morning."

"But not without Bess and George," Mr. Drew insisted.

Nancy called the cousins at once. Both were enthusiastic about accompanying the girl detective, although Bess as usual said she hoped there would be no danger involved.

"Oh, by the way, Ned was here," Nancy told her. "He's going to deliver our gifts to Honey, then take her and her mother to see Mr. Swenson."

"Good!" Bess giggled. "I see you're starting this friendship with Ned correctly—make your date work for you!" She hung up before Nancy could retort.

The following morning the girls drove to the

country store, made a few purchases, then asked if the stranger in the old car had ever come back.

"No, he never did, but he had no reason to," one of the clerks said. "The tank of that old crate was full to the brim, and there was enough food in the back seat to last the guy a month."

"Which way did he go?" Nancy asked.

The man pointed in a direction opposite to the one where the burned Raybolt home was located. After Nancy had received a full description of the old car, she followed the road it had taken.

Presently she said, "Girls, if you were coming along here and planning to hide, where would you go?"

"If I knew about that cobwebby cabin we saw I'd go there," George replied.

"But we were in it *after* Mr. Raybolt's disappearance," Nancy spoke up. "Nobody has been in it for a long time. Bess, what's your guess?"

"Another cabin. One that's closer. Maybe Mr. Raybolt has a small hunting lodge somewhere."

Nancy was driving very slowly now. Finally she said she was looking for a little-used side road. If there were tire tracks on it, she would see where they led.

Suddenly Nancy stopped. On her left was a narrow, grassy lane, almost obscured by overhanging trees. There were two distinct tire tracks.

"You're not going to drive in there?" Bess cried out. "Nancy, you'd ruin your car!"

"I guess you're right," Nancy conceded, "but I think we should investigate."

She parked, locked the ignition, and climbed out. The other girls followed. The woods road was rutty and full of stones.

"I hope we don't have to go far," said Bess presently. "These stones hurt my feet. We should have worn hiking boots."

Nancy forged ahead. The road went on and on, with no sign of a cabin, or the shabby car or its owner. After the girls had walked for fifteen minutes, Bess called for a rest period. They dropped to the ground.

"It's certainly quiet in here," George remarked. "You could hear a pin—oh!"

All three girls were startled by the distant buzz of a chain saw. As they listened, there came a tremendous crash.

"Timber!" exclaimed George, grinning.

"You're a little late with your warning. The tree's already fallen," Bess chided her cousin good-naturedly. "Well, I'm sure Mr. Raybolt isn't doing any lumbering if he's trying to hide, so let's go back."

Nancy felt that they were not a long way from the tree-cutting site. "Whoever is working there may have seen Mr. Raybolt or his old car. Let's find out," she said.

As the girls plodded on over the rough ground, the sounds of trees being felled grew louder. Finally they came to a spot where they could see a good distance ahead. A large area of the woods was being cleared for a housing development. They assumed that the entrance to it was at the far end, for in the distance they could see several new houses.

"There's a man who looks as if he might be the foreman," Nancy said, and walked toward a tall, husky young man. She introduced herself, then asked him if the lane was used by the real-estate developers.

"No, that's on someone else's property," he replied. "My name's Tim Murphy. I'm in charge of the clearing operation. Are you looking for someone?"

"Yes, a shabbily dressed man who has an ancient hot rod." Nancy grinned. "We thought he might be staying in a shack in these woods."

Tim Murphy's reply startled the girls. "I think your friend *was* here but left mysteriously. This development has been held up, and we just resumed work a couple of days ago. There's a little shack not far from here. It was empty, so whenever we had a downpour, my men and I used it for shelter.

"Two days ago we went there. What a surprise we got! A man came out with a shotgun and ordered us away! He was tall and thin, and his clothes were very shabby."

"Was there a car around?" George asked.

"Yes, a black crate that sure was beat up. Think this is the man you're looking for?"

"Yes," said Bess, "but if he has a shotgun, we're not going near him!"

Tim Murphy laughed. "You needn't worry. He's gone."

This revelation shattered Nancy's hope that her quest was nearing an end. "When did he leave?"

"During the night, and he hasn't come back. I have an idea he won't, either. I got the impression he wanted to be alone, and an expanding housing development is no place for a recluse. Say, do you mind telling me why you girls are interested in such a peculiar guy?"

They were spared the necessity of answering Murphy when a worker called him away. He went off hurriedly, and the girls started back to the lane. They were silent until they came to the spot where they had rested before.

"Do you think the man with the shotgun really was Mr. Raybolt?" George asked Nancy.

The young sleuth shrugged. "Your guess is as good as mine. One thing is sure. Whoever he was, the man acted as if he were guilty of something and didn't want strangers around."

"Which makes *me* think," said Bess, "that he *is* Raybolt. Nancy, we must give up trying to find him before he uses that shotgun—on us!"

"I might agree," Nancy replied, "if we were

certain. But our evidence is pretty slim. For the sake of the Swensons, I want to capture Mr. Raybolt before he can leave the country. I'm convinced now that he and his wife are in collusion. They're just waiting to collect his life insurance, which is probably large, and the fire insurance, then they'll meet in some foreign place."

George chuckled. "You know, it would serve that old cheat right if his wife collected the money and never met him! He couldn't do a thing about it without being caught."

Bess nodded in agreement. "And I wouldn't put it past that woman to play such a trick!"

When the girls reached the end of the lane, Bess announced that she thought they should have lunch before doing any more sleuthing.

"All right," Nancy agreed. Laughing, she added, "How about the Mapleton Inn?"

"And have Mrs. Raybolt bring the police to arrest you!" Bess protested with a giggle.

Nancy had noticed an attractive roadside restaurant on the outskirts of town and drove to it. As the girls ate, they discussed their next move.

"I'd like to call on Mr. Swenson," said Nancy, "and ask him if there's anything else in the diary that might be damaging evidence against Mr. Raybolt."

It was three o'clock before the girls arrived at headquarters. When Nancy made her request to the sergeant in charge of prisoners, she was told that Mr. Swenson had just been brought to one of the waiting rooms.

"His kid came to see him," the officer explained, "and we didn't want her to see him behind bars. We told Honey that her dad had to stay with us a while. His wife's there too. Are you special friends of theirs?"

"Yes."

"Okay, then." The sergeant called another officer, who took the girls into the waiting room. A policeman stood watching.

At once Honey bounded into Nancy's arms. "See, I have on all my new clothes!" she said proudly.

Mr. and Mrs. Swenson seemed very glad to see the visitors. The couple smiled pathetically and it was evident that Mrs. Swenson had spent a good deal of time crying. Her eyes were swollen and red. She looked pale and weary, as though she had slept little.

"Your kind friend Ned Nickerson brought Honey and me here. He will come back for us in an hour."

Joe Swenson looked haggard and worried. He brightened somewhat when Nancy told him that Baylor Weston was not only keeping his position at the factory for him, but that a promotion awaited the inventor.

"You're the only one who can help us," Mrs. Swenson said tearfully to Nancy. "We haven't enough money to engage a lawyer, and we have no well-to-do friends."

"If the case actually comes to trial, I know my father will defend Mr. Swenson without a fee," Nancy assured her. "However, I'm hopeful that we'll prove your husband's innocence before that time."

"The book you have may help," Mr. Swenson said guardedly.

Nancy nodded. She knew he meant the diary. It was still in her purse. She told herself, "I'll have the rest of it translated at once."

The girls remained a few minutes longer, then departed, realizing that the little family wished to be alone. When they reached the street, Nancy told her friends, "If Mr. Peterson's well enough, I'm going to see if he will read the diary. Let's go to a phone and find out."

CHAPTER XVIII

A Revealing Translation

THERE was an outdoor telephone booth at the entrance to a parking lot next to police headquarters. Nancy entered it and dialed the number of the Peterson bakery. To her delight, she learned that her old friend was home from the hospital and would be glad to see her.

When George heard this she said, "You're running a shuttle service between River Heights and Mapleton."

Bess giggled. "With side trips to Stanford and Sandy Creek."

"Don't plan on staying home long," Nancy warned them. "I may need you tonight."

"Tonight!" Bess exclaimed. "I was counting on giving myself a shampoo and—"

"Whatever it is," George interrupted, "the

Swenson-Raybolt mystery is more important. Well, I'll stick by you, Nancy."

"And I will, of course," Bess declared. "But please get this mystery solved soon, so I can catch up on a few things."

"Like what?" George asked.

"Well, I've postponed a nice date three times already," Bess said. "I was to go out with Jeff Allen tonight, but I'll put it off again. Nancy, where will we be going?"

Nancy said this would depend on what she learned from the diary.

When the girls reached River Heights, Nancy dropped off Bess and George at their homes, then drove to the Peterson bakery. She learned from the counter clerk that the owner was upstairs in his apartment, and the woman showed Nancy the stairway to the second floor.

The elderly convalescent was seated in an armchair and apologized for not rising to greet Nancy. She smiled, saying, "Mr. Peterson, it's wonderful to see you again, and how glad I am you're feeling better."

"Thank you, Nancy. Why, you're a young lady now!" He laughed. "I remember you as a little girl, always objecting to the ribbons Mrs. Gruen put in your hair. You especially liked my Swedish fruit tarts."

"Mm," said Nancy, smiling in recollection. "I

can almost taste the lingonberry ones now. They
were my favorite. Well, Mr. Peterson, I've come
to ask a favor of you. Would you translate a Swedish diary for me?"

"It would give me great pleasure. I am very
much interested in diaries. Many secrets of history have been unraveled by diaries that were uncovered some time after the writers' deaths."

"I never realized that," said Nancy.

"In many cases this is true of the personal
journals the famous people kept," the baker explained. "Take Queen Victoria of England, for
instance. Pictures of her and the complicated pol-
itics she was forced to play make her seem like a
very stern old lady. But she left a diary telling of
her life as a young queen and mother of small
children that gives a very different idea of her.
She was gay—loved to dance and give very ele-
gant parties."

"How interesting!"

"Then of course there were other diaries set
down by great men of history; for example,
George Washington's well-kept account of his
life. One section tells of a journey from Washington to Philadelphia which took five days! He also
told of a gift of mules to him from General Lafa-
yette for his farm.

"One of the most important diaries was that of
Christopher Columbus, who kept a record of his

entire journey from Palos in Spain to our continent. Did you know, Nancy, that when he saw the shores of Cuba he thought it was Japan?"

Nancy laughed. "I guess the old mariners made some amazing mistakes."

"What is more amazing is how they managed to get back home," said Mr. Peterson. "Some of the voyages must have seemed endless. I enjoyed reading about a schoolmaster who took a job as a private tutor with a family that was moving from Scotland to Virginia. It was a three-month voyage and all he received for tutoring the children was 'bed, board, washing, and five pounds' for the entire time!"

"How things have changed!" Nancy remarked.

She had listened in rapt attention to his recital of items in the old journals. Nancy wondered if Joe Swenson's up-to-date diary would prove to be as revealing about the writer's inner thoughts. A tingle of excitement came over her as she took the diary from her purse and handed it to Mr. Peterson.

The baker glanced through it before starting to read aloud. "The writer of this journal is an inventor, I see," he commented. "It's not a day-by-day account. Apparently he put down only the most important events."

Mr. Peterson began to translate. Much of what had been written was delightful and informative, but had no bearing on the Raybolt case.

After a while Nancy interrupted to say, "If you're becoming tired, please stop. I'll come back another time."

"Don't you worry, Nancy. I feel fine."

He read on. " 'Today,' " the diarist had written, " 'I went to see a man who sells inventions to big companies and shares the royalties with the inventors. His name is Raybolt. Tomorrow I shall take him my drawings and typed instructions for the electrochemical process and machine which will put a special ceramic finish on steel to resist high temperatures.' "

Mr. Peterson turned the page and translated a description of the meeting, during which Mr. Swenson had handed over everything to Felix Raybolt. He had been given a check for five hundred dollars and the verbal promise of a fifty-fifty royalty split in the future.

" 'Mr. Raybolt,' " Mr. Peterson translated, " 'is a very shrewd man. He confided to me that he didn't keep all his important papers and money in bank safe-deposit boxes. He has a secret hiding place in his house known to no one but himself. The—' "

"Just a minute!" Nancy cried out. "Please translate that part again about the secret hiding place!" To herself she added, "Maybe that's what Mr. Swenson meant when he said 'The book you have may help.' "

Mr. Peterson complied with Nancy's request,

then looked up and smiled. "You see a mystery here?"

"Indeed I do. And one that ought to be solved. Did you know that Mr. Raybolt's house burned to the ground and he has disappeared?"

"I had not heard," the baker replied. "But then I do not know this Felix Raybolt. Shall I read further?"

"Oh, please do."

Mr. Peterson went on. There were many references to the invention with some technical language about how the machine and the chemicals worked to produce the desired finish on metals.

"This is proof without a doubt that the invention is Mr. Swenson's," Nancy thought excitedly.

She listened carefully. The diary came to an end without any mention of a contract between the two men. Nancy was elated. Joe Swenson had a good case against Felix Raybolt! She was eager to talk over the whole matter with her father.

"Mr. Peterson," she said, taking the diary, "you've been a tremendous help in this mixed-up mystery. Thank you very much."

"I am glad to have been of assistance," the baker replied. "The reading was most enjoyable. This writer of the diary is well educated and clever." Mr. Peterson smiled. "But he does not sound like a very good businessman. I presume that is why he is in some kind of trouble."

"That's exactly it," Nancy answered.

*"Please translate that part again about the
secret hiding place!" Nancy asked*

"And you will get him out of the trouble," the baker said. He chuckled. "I just can't believe the little girl who loved cookies is now a detective!"

Nancy laughed, shook Mr. Peterson's hand fervently, and took her departure.

Wishing to see her father at once, she went directly to his office. Mr. Drew was about to leave, to be gone until later that evening.

"I can see you for about five minutes, Nancy," the lawyer said.

His daughter told Mr. Drew as quickly as possible what she had learned, and he agreed that the inventor had a good chance of winning his case—if Mr. Raybolt could be found.

"So far the police haven't a clue to his whereabouts, Nancy. I believe you came nearer to capturing him than anyone else has. It's too bad he moved out of that cabin."

"And worse that he has disappeared into thin air," Nancy replied. "But I'm not giving up!"

"That's the spirit," her father said affectionately. "Well, best of luck! And when you see Mr. Swenson, tell him not to worry."

Nancy drove home slowly as she tried to figure out the puzzle. When she reached the house, Hannah Gruen was taking a few minutes' rest and sipping a cup of tea. Nancy joined her and told of the most recent happenings.

"My goodness," said the housekeeper, "you've

done several days' work in one! Now you must relax."

Nancy hardly touched her own cup of tea. She sat staring into space, and understanding Mrs. Gruen did not interrupt the young sleuth's train of thought.

Suddenly Nancy cried, "I've just figured it out!"

"Figured what out?"

"How to trap Felix Raybolt!"

CHAPTER XIX

Setting a Trap

NANCY told Hannah Gruen her plan. She believed that Felix Raybolt was hiding somewhere near the ruined estate, perhaps in the dense woods which adjoined the property, and she proposed to watch the place for a return visit.

"It's said that a criminal always returns to the scene of his crime," she declared. "And he has a special reason, besides—to get something out of the secret hiding place. Up till now, I understand, police guards have been stationed on the grounds day and night. The special investigators from out of town expected to finish their examination of the ruins today, and the guards would no longer be necessary."

"What do you plan to do?" Mrs. Gruen asked.

"Bess and George and I will watch for him tonight. We may waste our time, but I have a feeling—I can't explain it—that we'll catch him near the burned house."

"It sounds risky, Nancy. How about taking a man with you?"

"Dad won't be home to supper. He'll be out for the evening." After a pause Nancy added, "Maybe I can get Ned Nickerson."

"Please do that."

Nancy telephoned Ned's house but there was no answer. "I'll stop there when I get to Mapleton," she told Hannah.

When George received Nancy's call, she was intrigued to hear about the secret hiding place where Mr. Raybolt kept valuable papers.

"Where do you suppose it is—or was?" George asked.

"If it's still intact," Nancy replied, "there's only one spot for a hiding place—behind the stones of the cellar wall. Even if Mr. Raybolt doesn't show up, I'd like to try to find it. So come dressed for some digging!"

Nancy made the same request of Bess and added that she would pick her up in forty-five minutes.

"Fine," said Bess. "That'll give me time to eat and get dressed. I'll be ready."

Finally the girls were on their way to Mapleton.

"It's going to be pretty dark tonight," Bess commented. "There'll be no moon."

"So much the better," Nancy declared. "Mr. Raybolt probably wouldn't venture to return if he thought there would be any danger of his being detected."

"Your plan sounds dangerous to me," Bess remarked. "What if Mr. Raybolt should come and make trouble?"

"We'd be three to one," Nancy returned. "Of course it would be better if we had a man along. I'm going to stop at Ned's house and see if he can come with us."

"Good!"

The sun was sinking low when Nancy swung into Mapleton. The girls stopped at the Nickerson residence which was on their route, but were disappointed to learn that Ned had not returned home after driving Mrs. Swenson and Honey to Sandy Creek.

"Who knows—maybe he's off hunting for Foxy Felix," Nancy said to her friends. "I'll leave a note for him, and if he should get back in time, he might follow us to the estate."

She quickly wrote a message and gave it to Ned's mother. Mrs. Nickerson promised to deliver it the moment her son came home.

As they drove away from the Nickerson home, Bess said nervously, "I have a feeling something dreadful is going to happen tonight. It wouldn't be so bad if there only were other houses close by, but they're so far away, the neighbors wouldn't hear us even if we screamed for help."

"Calm down," Nancy advised. "Three strong,

capable girls like ourselves shouldn't need any help."

"I'd be a match for Foxy Felix myself," George boasted. "Look at *my* arm muscles. I assure you I haven't wasted all the time I spent in the gym."

Dusk was just settling when the girls came within sight of the burned mansion. The Raybolt estate looked unpleasantly lonely. Even George felt less inclined to joke as she realized that within a few moments it would be dark.

Nancy drove past the estate and hid the convertible in a dense clump of trees.

"We'll leave the car here," she said, "and go quietly up the driveway."

The girls armed themselves with flashlights, a pick, and two lightweight shovels. Then they went cautiously along the road and turned into the estate. No one came to challenge them as they reached the ruined house. A few charred beams which had not fallen to the ground stood like sentinels guarding the wreckage. In the dimness the girls could easily imagine that they were ghostly figures.

"This is going to be spookier than I figured," Bess chattered nervously. "Nancy, you do have the wildest ideas."

The girl detective did not reply to this. When she was fairly certain no one else was around, she turned on her flashlight and played it on the stone walls of the house's foundation. Nancy realized it would be a herculean task to move the debris away to inspect them. Nevertheless, she set the light on a pile of rubble and began to shovel away a heap of plaster.

"What do you expect to find?" George asked, turning on her flashlight and setting it down. "And tell me how I can help."

"A safe," Nancy answered. "And how about you girls taking turns with the pick and shovel? The other one act as lookout."

Bess posted herself as guard while the others worked. Nancy and George uncovered several feet of wall but found no loose stones or anything indicating a section to open. The stones were tightly cemented.

Suddenly Bess whispered hoarsely, "Put out the lights! I hear someone coming!"

The flashes were clicked off and the three girls crouched down. They could hear nothing now.

"I'm sure I wasn't mistaken," Bess said.

"I believe we had better quit this work and hide," said Nancy. "If Mr. Raybolt is coming, he'll probably be here soon."

"Maybe he's the person I heard," Bess whispered.

"All the more reason for us to pretend to be leaving in case he's watching us," George spoke up.

The girls left the ruins without turning on their lights, stumbling and falling over the debris. They went down the driveway, but before reaching the end, Nancy said, "Let's leave the tools here, go into the woods, and sneak back toward the ruins."

They hid the pick and shovels and retraced their steps. Nancy found a place behind a clump of bushes only a short distance from the ruins. The shrubs concealed the girls, yet disclosed a view of the driveway and the woods. Nancy and her friends settled themselves as comfortably as possible. But from the first, insects made it plain that they resented the intrusion.

A half hour passed, then an hour. The girls were startled several times as twigs crackled or dead limbs of trees crashed in the breeze.

"The bugs have nearly eaten me up," Bess complained, "and my back feels as though it were broken."

"You'll become paralyzed after another hour or so." Nancy grinned.

"How long do you propose staying here?" George demanded. "It must be almost midnight now."

"It isn't ten o'clock yet." Nancy laughed.

"Well, I don't think Mr. Raybolt is coming or he'd have been here by this time," Bess said sleepily. "Why don't we go home?"

"I want to stay a while longer," Nancy returned quietly.

Again the girls became silent. Bess and George,

having accustomed themselves to their hiding place, stretched out and left Nancy to keep watch. They were no longer nervous or afraid—only weary of an adventure which had gone stale.

Presently George became very quiet and then fell asleep. Bess's eyes closed, too, and soon she was in a deep sleep.

How long the cousins slept, they had no idea. But suddenly they were awakened by a scream, and the sound of running feet on the driveway.

"Nancy!" cried George, jumping up. "What has happened?"

There was no answer.

"Nancy!" called Bess, grabbing George by the arm.

Still there was no answer, and the two girls realized that their friend was no longer with them. Where was she? Who had screamed? Who was coming up the road in such haste?

CHAPTER XX

A Surprising Victory

WHILE the cousins had been asleep, Nancy had taken matters into her own hands. Her mind had been too active for her to feel sleepy. As she watched, first the woods, then the driveway, then the burned house, she suddenly became aware of footsteps.

"Maybe that's Ned," she thought hopefully.

The masculine figure was still too far away for Nancy to be able to discern who it could be. While she waited with bated breath, the man paused. She was about to awaken Bess and George when it occurred to her that they might speak aloud and warn the oncoming figure of their presence.

As the man turned toward the burned house, Nancy was in a quandary. She did not dare rouse her friends, yet she wanted to follow the intruder. She must find out who he was—Ned, come to help her, an inquisitive neighbor, or Felix Raybolt.

Leaving her friends, Nancy began to follow the man. Stealthily she crept nearer the ruins, dodging from tree to tree. She was glad there was no moon, for the darkness afforded protection.

When she was only a few feet away from the man, Nancy paused. He turned on a flashlight. This was not Ned Nickerson. From descriptions of the estate owner and from numerous newspaper photographs of him, Nancy felt certain that the tall, thin figure must be Felix Raybolt! He was carrying a shovel.

Suddenly he scrambled over the rubble and began to dig vigorously in the cellar wall some distance from where Nancy had been working.

"So that's where the secret hiding place is," thought the young detective.

She watched excitedly as Mr. Raybolt uncovered a group of stones in the foundation wall. He removed them, opened the door of a safe beyond, and pulled out a stack of papers. To Nancy's horror, he laid them down and set a match to the sheaf.

"It's evidence against him!" Nancy said to herself. "He can't destroy it!"

Instantly Nancy sprang forward. She grabbed the shovel and beat out the flames. At the same time she cried, "Mr. Felix Raybolt, you can't burn those papers!"

The man had started violently and staggered backward. Nancy caught him by the arm, saying, "Why have you been hiding?"

Almost at once, Mr. Raybolt recovered from the shock of the unexpected encounter, and jerked himself free. For an instant he looked at Nancy in blank amazement.

"A snooper, eh?" he sneered.

Without warning he grabbed both his flashlight and her own. He turned and started to run across the grounds. "Get out of my way! Mind your own business!" he warned.

Nancy darted after him, but he definitely had the advantage of being familiar with the area. Her only chance to capture him lay in the possibility of his turning toward the place where she had left Bess and George. She must arouse them. Nancy did not know what Raybolt might do if she made an outcry, but she had to take that chance.

"Help! Help!" she screamed.

Bess and George, having heard the shrill cries for help, and approaching footsteps, were now convinced Nancy had uttered the cries and that she was in danger.

"Oh, what shall we do?" asked Bess. "The screams seemed to come from near the ruins."

"Sh!" George warned. "Those footsteps coming up the driveway! Maybe it's someone who can help us!"

This remark electrified Bess, who turned on

her flash and rushed frantically ahead. She was the first to reach two men running up the driveway.

"Mr. Drew! Ned Nickerson!" the cousins cried in relief.

"Where's Nancy?" the men asked together.

"We don't know," Bess gasped. "We heard her scream—over by the ruins."

The men dashed past the girls, Ned in the lead. Bess and George started after them.

"Help! Help!" came Nancy's scream again, but this time it was nearer.

Suddenly a man's figure burst from a clump of shrubs at the bend in the driveway. He saw the approaching group too late to stop. He could not turn, for Nancy appeared directly behind him. He veered off to the lawn.

"Hold on there!" Mr. Drew commanded sharply.

"Dad!" Nancy cried out, and an instant later she recognized the second figure. "Ned!"

Felix Raybolt was easily captured. The appearance of the two men convinced the estate owner that his game was up, and he made little protest as they led him to Carson Drew's sedan.

"Nancy, you girls had better come with us," Mr. Drew suggested. "You can return and pick up your car later." They agreed readily.

"Where are you taking me?" Raybolt muttered, as he got into the sedan.

"To jail," Mr. Drew told him tersely.

"To jail?" the prisoner shrieked. "I haven't done anything!"

"Maybe not, but an innocent man is being held there in connection with your disappearance. You *must* exonerate Joe Swenson at once from having had anything to do with your absence or with the fire."

"Swenson?" echoed the captured man. "He—"

Raybolt broke off and slumped down in the seat. He looked sick and beaten. His face was grimy and unshaven, and his clothing torn and stained.

"How in the world did you and Dad get here at the psychological moment?" Nancy asked Ned.

"Well—I'd been gone from home since morning," Ned explained. "This evening I drove to River Heights to see you. Mrs. Gruen told me you had gone to Mapleton and said she thought I was with you. I telephoned Mother from your house and she gave me your message."

Mr. Drew added, "I returned home just as Ned was leaving. When I heard what you were doing I decided I'd better come along."

At the jail Foxy Felix did not even appear to be flustered about the situation. When questioned by the officials, he admitted that he had had an appointment with Joe Swenson but said that he had been outside the house at the time of the explosion.

"Isn't it true that you had explosives illegally stored in your cellar?" Nancy asked him.

Raybolt nodded. He claimed the explosion and fire had been accidental. When asked about his disappearance, he gave an evasive explanation. He said that he had been stunned at first, then had staggered off into the woods.

"And vanished," said Carson Drew. "You carry heavy life and fire insurance, I presume, Mr. Raybolt. Your wife could have collected the money, and met you later in some faraway place."

The telltale flush on Raybolt's face told the lawyer that Nancy's and his supposition had probably hit its mark, but Raybolt confessed nothing. They judged that Mapleton *had* become too unfriendly a place for Foxy Felix. His enemies were numerous, and he no doubt lived in constant fear of physical harm. The fire had given him an opportunity to slip away quietly.

"Guess we can't hold him," the captain told the Drews. "This clears Swenson beyond a doubt. Sorry we arrested him, Miss Drew, but you must admit the evidence pointed his way."

Joe Swenson was brought into the room. He was overjoyed about being freed, and at first could scarcely believe the good news. Tears came to his eyes as he thanked Nancy and her friends for all they had done.

"It's a shame that Felix Raybolt can't be held,"

Nancy said. "Isn't there *any* charge to keep him here?"

"I'm afraid not," her father returned. "Everyone knows the man has swindled people, including my client, but we have no proof. We need papers, letters—"

Suddenly Nancy grabbed her father's arm. "I may be able to produce them!" she said excitedly, and told about the papers which Raybolt had tried to burn but she had managed to save.

"Excellent," said Mr. Drew, as Bess, George, and Ned gasped in astonishment. "We'll go out there at once with an officer if Captain Johnson agrees."

The captain called a lieutenant and said that the man would accompany them to the burned estate. Mr. Raybolt, he added, would have to remain at headquarters to await the arrival of the papers.

The others hurried outside and drove off in a squad car. When they reached the ruins, Nancy pointed out the exact location of the safe. The police lieutenant quickly gathered up the records that Raybolt had started to burn, also some papers which the officer found in the safe. When the Drews and their friends reached headquarters, they were amazed to find that Mrs. Raybolt had arrived. She was admonishing her husband not to admit anything.

Captain Johnson handed the papers to Mr. Drew. "Please look at these," he requested. "If they have any bearing on this case—"

Felix Raybolt jumped from his chair. "Don't read them! I admit I paid small sums to inventors and promised royalties I never sent, though I sold their ideas for large amounts. I'll give restitution to every one of them!"

"Felix! Felix!" his wife screamed. "Don't give in!" She glared at Nancy. "Oh—look at all the trouble you've caused!"

Raybolt appeared not to hear her. "I'll pay everyone even if it takes my last cent! I'll do anything if only you won't send me to prison!"

"Don't do it! Don't do it!" Mrs. Raybolt pleaded. "We'll be ruined!"

"We'll be ruined if I don't," her husband muttered, "because I'll have to go to jail."

Mrs. Raybolt sank into a chair, covered her face with her hands, and began to sob. For an instant Nancy felt sorry for her, then changed her mind, as the woman burst out:

"We had the whole thing so well planned. No loopholes. Then this Nancy Drew has to come along and spoil our lives."

Nancy, her father, their friends, and the police captain looked at Mrs. Raybolt in astonishment. The officer leaned forward and asked, "Are you admitting that you and your husband planned this whole unscrupulous plot?"

"Keep quiet!" Raybolt stormed.

But the damage had been done. Little by little a full confession was obtained from the husband and wife about the plot they had devised to pile up a fortune from insurance, then vanish.

Raybolt finally admitted that he had rigged up a television set on the first floor to trigger the explosion by remote control. He had planned that it would go off when Joe Swenson arrived for the appointment.

"But Swenson was twenty minutes early," Mr. Raybolt growled, "so I had to go ahead and cause the explosion without getting the papers out of the safe. I knew I could come back later for them."

Further questioning proved that Mrs. Raybolt was responsible for having the two detectives track down the inventor and put the blame on him.

At the end of the session, everyone in the room showed complete disgust for the Raybolts.

"All their conniving at the expense of other people," Nancy thought.

Both the Raybolts were held. They were allowed to telephone for legal counsel, but even before the lawyer arrived, the husband asked for a checkbook from Mrs. Raybolt's purse and wrote out a check for several thousand dollars to the order of Joe Swenson.

"If you'll look among those papers Nancy

Drew saved," the estate owner said, "you'll find one that's a receipt for the sale of his invention to the Streeter Corporation."

Mr. Drew looked at the receipt and commented that the amount of the check was five hundred dollars less than the sum on the receipt.

"I received five hundred from Mr. Raybolt in cash," Joe Swenson spoke up. Then, without smiling, he added, "Thank you, Mr. Raybolt, for this check."

Mr. Drew, meanwhile, had continued looking through the papers Nancy had rescued. He frowned angrily, but said nothing until he came to a bulging envelope which he opened.

"These are the plans stolen from my client, Mr. Simpson," he remarked. "I will take them, Mr. Raybolt. And, Captain Johnson, I think you had better keep the rest of these papers to see that the other inventors are properly reimbursed."

"I'll certainly see that they are," the officer declared.

All the visitors but the Raybolts left headquarters. Ned offered to take the still-stunned Joe Swenson home in order to break the good news to his wife. Honey, of course, would be asleep.

"Suppose you come to dinner at our house tomorrow for a victory celebration, all of you," Nancy invited. "Ned, could you—"

"Yes, I'll gladly drive the Swensons over," he said.

Bess chortled, "We wouldn't miss it for the world!" and George nodded vigorously.

The following day was an exceedingly happy one at the Drew home. The Swensons wore broad grins, and Honey's mother said, "We owe all our happiness to you, Nancy."

"I think you owe it to the fact that your husband dropped the diary," Nancy said, smiling.

"Yes," said George. "If it hadn't been for the clue Nancy found in it, she never could have located the owner and helped bring you all together."

As the gala dinner ended, Mr. Swenson mentioned that Baylor Weston was promoting him to a responsible position in the experimental division of the factory at a large salary.

"That's marvelous," said Nancy.

"You have been so kind to us," Mrs. Swenson spoke up, "that we want to show our appreciation in a more material way."

She presented each of the girls with a tissue-wrapped package. "It isn't much," she said apologetically.

"Indeed it is!" Nancy cried, unwrapping a beautiful purse.

As she opened it, the girl detective found a note inside. The message read: "Will you please keep my signet ring to remind you of your adventure and of our deep gratitude for all you have done for us. Joe Swenson."

"I'd love to, of course," Nancy said, a little catch in her throat. "The ring has meant a great deal to you. Now it will to me."

Bess and George likewise received purses and Ned a wallet. They thanked the donors heartily. A short time later the inventor and his family left, after promising to call frequently on Nancy and her father.

The young detective felt a glow of pleasure as always when she made lasting friends of people she had helped. But she did not know in what strange way this would occur soon again. Much to her amazement, in her next adventure, *Nancy's Mysterious Letter,* she was to help someone with a name like her own who was in great trouble.

"It really was a gorgeous party!" Bess sighed blissfully. "Such fun!"

"Say," said Ned, "I have a notion to start a diary of my own!"

"Why don't you?" Nancy asked lightly.

She became conscious that Ned's eyes were looking straight at her. "I will if I can fill most of the pages with entries of dates with you."

Nancy evaded the question. "I enjoyed your help in solving the Swenson mystery. Maybe we'll soon find another one we can work on together."